STEELE: THE VIOLENT PEACE

Also by the same author and available in the NEL series:

EDGE: THE LONER
EDGE: TEN THOUSAND DOLLARS AMERICAN
EDGE: APACHE DEATH
EDGE: KILLER'S BREED
EDGE: BLOOD ON SILVER
EDGE: THE BLUE, THE GREY AND THE RED
EDGE: CALIFORNIA KILLING
EDGE: SEVEN OUT OF HELL
EDGE: BLOODY SUMMER
EDGE: VENGEANCE IS BLACK
EDGE: SIOUX UPRISING
EDGE: THE BIGGEST BOUNTY

Steele: The Violent Peace

George G. Gilman

NEW ENGLISH LIBRARY
TIMES MIRROR

For F. T. H. who always knew things would be this good.

*

FIRST NEL PAPERBACK EDITION APRIL 1974

*

NEL Books are published by
New English Library Limited from Barnard's Inn, Holborn, London, E.C.1.
Made and printed in Great Britain by Hunt Barnard Printing Ltd., Aylesbury, Bucks.

45001769 9

CHAPTER ONE

IN Washington the night of Friday, April 14, 1865 was cold. Damp mist curled insubstantial grey tentacles into the nooks and crannies of the re-united nation's capital. It muffled sounds from far off but seemed to amplify the weary footfalls of the blue-uniformed soldiers patrolling the sidewalk outside Ford's Theatre on Tenth Street.

Inside the building, President Abraham Lincoln and his entourage looked down from the vantage point of a box, enjoying the performance of *Our American Cousin.* The remainder of the audience divided their attention between the stage and the occupants of the box. Some were merely curious to catch a glimpse of the nation's number one citizen in a brief period of relaxation after the gruelling years of anxiety caused by the War Between the States. Others showed concern at how sick he looked. A handful were awe-struck at being in such close proximity to the country's leader. Four waited for the fatal bullet to be fired.

Outside in the cold night a captain of the Washington Cavalry Police cast a nervous eye over the expanding group of sightseers that had begun to form on the street. The Appomattox surrender was only five days old and the fires of hatred still burned bright in countless Southern hearts.

Far off, over towards the Capitol, a clock chimed and the police captain checked his vest pocket watch. It was nine forty-five.

'Best move the President's carriage up, sir,' he suggested to an artillery captain.

The army officer was blowing on his cupped hands. 'Clock sounds closer somehow,' he said.

Both men glanced up between the hissing globes of street lights and saw bright pinpricks of stars, each with a blurred halo.

'Mist's clearing,' the police captain commented with a nod. 'It'll make our job a little easier.'

The army man blew on his hands again, as he turned and approached the presidential carriage. The bored guards stiffened and a sergeant major threw up a salute, then nodded several times as he listened to the officer's instructions. The transport for the President and Mrs Lincoln was moved forward and the carriages for the other dignitaries closed up behind it. Finding their view of the theatre entrance obscured, the sightseers shuffled along the sidewalk on the opposite side of the street. Movement alleviated their coldness a little. Anticipation that the activity in front of the theatre meant President Lincoln would shortly appear was more warming.

'I know a place over on E. Street where they got women!' a man shouted with drunken excitement.

Those in the centre section of the group of watchers turned towards the source of the sudden raucousness, eager for distraction to break the monotony of the wait. The double swing doors of Elmer's Barroom had swung wide and three happily drunk soldiers staggered out. There also emerged a splash of bright light and a comforting waft of warm air heavy with the smell of hard liquor and cigar smoke. Some of the men in the crowd licked their lips in a moment of wishful thinking, but each found himself in the unrelenting grip of a wife's steady hold.

The trio of soldiers – all privates wearing the insignia of a Pennsylvania Rifles company – pulled up short and blinked at the sea of faces before them.

'Which one of you guys is famous?' the smallest soldier asked, and belched loudly.

'You didn't have to do this, folks,' the man who knew about the bordello announced with a limp bow that almost toppled him. 'We had a little help in winning the war.'

'What's the disturbance over there?' a voice called loudly from the other side of the street.

The three soldiers glanced nervously at each other, coming close to sobering up. They had all been in the army long enough to recognise the voice of authority without needing to see insignia.

'Let's move it, right quick,' the eldest of the trio said in an urgent whisper.

He lowered himself into a crouch and scampered away behind the cover of the sightseers.

'I smell a bad smell,' the short youngster hissed.

'Must be an officer,' the third one said sagely.

Then they followed the example of the first man to escape, veering to left and right on unsteady legs. Some of the watchers laughed. Others made throaty sounds of disapproval. But soon it was quiet again, except for low-voiced complaints against the cold For the ball of warmth which had exploded from the bar with the soldiers was long gone, dissipated through the frosty night air as it wafted in from the north-east in the wake of the mist.

There was warmth to spare inside the bar. It was a long room with a scarred wooden bar running the entire length of the rear wall. The area in front of the bar was liberally featured with circular tables surrounded by ladder-back chairs. Only one of the tables was in use, occupied by four business-suited men in middle years playing penny-ante five card draw. They stayed, drew and raised with soft-voiced expressions of intent. Smoke from their cigars drifted slowly upwards to hang in a blue-grey pall among the cob-webbed beams across the ceiling.

Beneath a nearby table, an elderly drunk with a toothless mouth and deeply scored skin snored in a contented sleep, an empty gin bottle clutched lovingly to his chest. The barman, big broad and ugly with the expression of one who had not slept in many nights, cast resentful glances towards the old man, but made no move to throw him out. Instead, he leaned against a shelf of bottles and wiped wet glasses with mechanical monotony. The brooding eyes in his ugly face did not even have to guide his thick-fingered hands as they picked up a wet glass and set down a dry one.

He had two other customers, both standing at the bar within three feet of each other, but not talking. One was about sixty, short, slightly built and impeccably dressed in an expensively cut blue suit with a black cape draped over his slim shoulders. His kindly, clean-shaven face wore a slight smile and he gave the impression that all was right in his particular world.

He suddenly drained the heeltap of liquid in his shot glass and broadened the perpetual smile as he looked along the bar.

'Another bourbon, if you'll be so kind, bartender,' he called. His voice betrayed a Deep South origin.

The ugly man behind the bar sighed and interrupted his chore to reach for a bottle of whiskey from the shelf behind him. He dawdled down towards his customer as if the last thing he wanted to do was serve drinks. He tilted the bottle over the empty glass and again he did not have to concentrate on what he was doing. Instead, he fastened his sullen stare upon the face of the second customer standing at the bar. This was a tall, haggard-faced man with receding hair and a thick moustache. He wore a black suit which looked too large for him. It was crumpled and stained; as ill-used as the man who wore it.

The bartender knew automatically when to stop pouring and he did not spill a drop. He accepted payment without thanks and thrust the money into a deep pocket at the front of his leather apron.

'Is that clock correct, sir?'

The bartender's black eyes flicked over the smiling face of his customer and glanced at the grimy dial of the big clock hung on the far wall. The hands pointed out the time of four minutes to ten.

'Ain't never known it be a second out since I bought this place,' he replied grudingly, and looked pointedly back at the other man on the patron's side of the bar.

'Should have been met here at nine-thirty,' the dapper little man said cheerfully, raising his fresh drink. 'Still, I've waited almost five years for him. Guess thirty minutes or so won't make any difference. When a man gets to be my age – '

The haggard-looking man at his side had seemed impervious to his surroundings. For a full quarter of an hour he had remained like a statue, not touching the glass of beer standing between his splayed hands, his wide eyes staring at the row of bottles on the shelf behind the bar. He had certainly been unaware of the bartender's blatant interest in him. But suddenly he whirled, like a machine powered into action. His hands balled into fists, matching the tension in his face: and one of them collided with the dapper man's upraised elbow. The contents of the glass were hurled across the drinker's shoulder, splashing on to the cape.

'I'm sorry!' the younger man exclaimed, embarrassment fusing with anxiety in the lines of his face as he leaned across to brush ineffectually at the damp stain. 'Let me get you another drink. . . . I do beg your pardon. . . . You called attention to the time. . . . I'll be late for an appointment. Please, I must – '

The older man's surprise was fleeting, and the smile returned. 'Quite all right, young man. Damage is only slight. Good thing, maybe. Had enough. Don't want to be in my cups when my . . . '.

His voice trailed away as he realised the man who had spilled the drink was no longer listening. He had completed the pivot and was striding purposefully between the tables towards the doors. A slight glimmer of satisfaction showed behind the sullenness of the bartender's eyes as he watched his customer go from sight.

The dapper man clicked his tongue against the back of his teeth and sighed as he jerked out a silk handkerchief to mop at the stain on his cape. 'These young fellers,' he muttered. 'All hassle and hurry.' Then he shook his head reflectively and glanced towards the doors, but the man had left. 'Got a feeling I've seen that one before somewhere.'

'If you go to the theatre much, maybe you did,' the bartender answered with a growling tone. 'Actor. Name's John Wilkes Booth.'

CHAPTER TWO

THE clock over towards the Capitol had finished striking the hour of ten when John Wilkes Booth stepped softly into Box Seven of Ford's Theatre and approached the back of the horse-hair rocker in which the President sat. The derringer was already in his hand and he levelled it to point at a spot midway between his victim's left ear and the top of his spine. As a burst of laughter rose from the audience, the assassin squeezed the trigger of the tiny gun.

'It's done, let's go.'

The English voice, speaking in a whisper, dragged the eyes of three men away from the stage. They were seated, close to the Englishman, near the rear of the theatre within easy reach of the exit doors. Whilst the remainder of the audience continued to chortle at the comic dialogue spoken by the on-stage actors, this quartet glanced furtively up at the shadowy movements in Box Seven. Then they rose and filed towards the exit.

'Revenge for the South!' Booth shouted hysterically, then whirled and raced from the box.

The actors faltered in their lines and, as a piercing scream rose from the State Box, hundreds of startled playgoers swung around to look for the cause of the interruption.

'Water!'

'The President's been shot!'

Another woman screamed, and slumped from her seat in a dead faint.

'Is he dead?'

'Please, get us some water?'

'Is he dead?'

The majority of people in the theatre seemed to have been struck dumb, paralysed by the shooting. So that the pleas and questions yelled by a few sounded much like dramatic lines spoken before an awed audience.

'It was Booth. I saw him running. With a gun!'

'Stop him! Stop that man!'

Suddenly, the mass numbness was over. The entire theatre was filled with wails, screams and shouts, each counter-acting another so that nothing could be heard clearly. Then hysteria forced its victims into movement and there was a scrambling rush for the doors.

The four men who had been first to leave stood in the theatre lobby, smoking newly-lit cigarettes, in the calm manner of innocent playgoers who had stepped out for a breath of fresh air. Their appearance had captured the fleeting attention of the police and army captains standing by the carriages, but the officers had immediately lost interest when they realised the opening doors did not signal the end of the performance.

But suddenly the panicked mass exodus exploded in the lobby. An elderly man, his face as white as a sheet, was urged along at the head of the throng.

'The President!' he screamed at the four men. 'The President's been shot!'

As the bringer of the news rushed out on to the street, repeating the same two phrases, his voice rising in pitch with every word, the four found themselves caught up in the crowd pressing in pursuit.

'He's not dead!' a woman wailed. 'He can't be dead.'

While policemen and soldiers struggled to assimilate the awful announcement, the crowd of sightseers surged forward from the opposite sidewalk.

'Murderer!' a man shouted. 'Assassin! Stop the assassin!'

'Mommy, mommy!' a small girl wailed from deep within the pressing crowd. 'I wanna go home.'

'Who did it?' a woman demanded to know, tears streaming down her face. 'Who was it?'

'It's the Johnnie Rebs!' a man shouted in response. 'They've got Lincoln.'

The four men who had left the theatre early found themselves thrust out into the street. They, and many more, were shoved viciously aside as police and military personnel struggled to get inside the seething lobby.

The Englishman, a head taller than the others, launched a spiteful kick at the legs of a soldier who had levered him aside with a rifle stock. The soldier was prevented from falling by the mass of the people, but when he whirled to locate his attacker, the man was gone, he and his three companions elbowing their way to wards the lights of Elmer's Barroom.

'In the head, goddamnit!' a fuming old timer bellowed. 'Right in the back of the head. Blood everywhere.'

'He's not dead! I saw him when they lifted him. He was breathing.'

A hundred hopeful faces turned towards the giver of this news.

On the edge of the crowd, a young man with only one arm stared at the milling people with a fiery gaze. 'I'm glad the nigger-lover's dead,' he muttered.

Fear leapt to his face and he stepped quickly backwards as the Englishman struggled clear of the crowd. The Englishman smiled at the one-armed youngster. 'Amen to that, old son,' he said softly, and turned to look for his companions.

As the three forced themselves clear, an old black man stretched his arms high into the air. 'They shot him!' he cried. 'It was all for nothing.'

His fat wife dropped to her knees in the street and clasped her hands together. 'He can't die. God won't let him die!'

The Englishman and his three followers stepped up on to the sidewalk in front of the bar and looked across the heads of struggling crowds, swelling to enormous proportions as news-hungry people came running from every direction.

'Guards!' a distraught doctor yelled. 'Guards – clear the passage!'

Soldiers and civilians linked arms in two lines, enforcing a corridor through the press of sightseers.

'God Almighty, get him to the White House!' a man implored as four artillerymen appeared, the limp form of the President slung between them.

'He'd die on the way,' a second doctor responded, waving aside the captain who stepped forward to jerk open the door of the state carriage.

The captain swung around and slapped the Colt from his holster, waving it in the faces of the shocked people on the other side of the carriage. 'Out of the way, you sons of bitches!' he demanded.

The crowd parted and the captain led the soldiers with their burden, followed by the doctors, out on to Tenth Street. A woman stood in an open doorway, craning to see what was happening in front of the theatre.

'That house!' one of the doctors instructed, squeezing between the soldiers and the crowd, then angling towards the opposite sidewalk. 'He must be allowed to rest.'

The woman swallowed hard and fell back before the advance of the doctor and the wan-faced men behind him. President Lincoln was carried into the house in which he would die.

'He looks bad,' the Englishman said with mock gravity, keeping his voice low as a silence settled over the crowd.

'Reckon he'll get worse?' one of his companions asked in the same tone.

'Let's go and drink to it,' another suggested.

A third pushed open the doors and they filed into the fetid warmth of the bar. It was a little more crowded than when Booth had left to shoot the President. The dapper man with a damp shoulder was still the sole customer standing at the bar, having decided to risk another bourbon. The drunk continued to snore beneath the table, clutching at the empty bottle as though it was a life-line. The poker game had ended, the cards in disarray on the table, the players having switched from beer to whiskey to try to calm shattered nerves. But now several other tables were occupied, by men in pairs, trios and quartets: all of them drinking in quiet contemplation.

'Terrible thing,' the dapper man muttered, sipping his whiskey, his face heavy with sadness in vivid contrast to his earlier good humour. 'That's a great man, one hell of a great man.'

The bartender looked anxiously up from his glass-washing chore towards the newcomers.

'Hey, Elmer,' the Englishman called. 'Service, please.'

He led the others to the bar and they all bellied up to it, hooking boot heels over the brass rail. The dapper man looked at them with a melancholy expression and nodded. He drew no response.

'Four whiskeys,' the Englishman requested.

He was a tall, slim man in his late twenties, with handsome, evenly-tanned features out of which blue eyes looked with an air of superior self confidence. He was dressed in a well-cut suit with a gold watch chain slung across his velvet vest. There was something military in the neatness of his dress and his upright bearing.

'Coming right up, Mr Carstairs,' Elmer replied with a hint of deference, quickly setting out four shot glasses and tilting a bottle over them.

'You hear what happened over at the theatre, mister?'

The old man who had been hit so badly by the tragedy at the theatre realised he was being addressed and turned to look at the newcomer standing next to him. 'We heard the shouting,' he answered, and gestured with a motion of his head. 'Then some gentlemen came in and told us about it. Terrible thing.'

'Here you are, Jack,' Carstairs said, sliding one of the brimming glasses along the bartop.

Jack Logan was twenty-two, short and fat with a round, unintelligent face. His suit was too small and looked like a hand-me-down. As he surveyed the man in the cape beside him, he pulled absently at the crotch of his tight-fitting pants, trying to relieve the pressure.

'Here's to the capture of the bastard that did it to Lincoln.'

The speaker, who lifted his glass and tipped down the drink at a swallow, was named Edward Binns. He was a foot shorter than Carstairs, but his build was broader. His age was the same as the obvious leader of the group, but his face was more ravaged by the elements and his meaty hands – showing traces of grimed-in dirt – suggested he was a manual worker. Although his suit fitted him well, he nonetheless seemed to be uncomfortable in it, as if more used to less formal attire. He had a shock of black hair on which a derby was balanced precariously.

'Right,' the fourth member of the group grunted.

Like Carstairs and Binns, Frank Monahan was in his late twenties, but that was the only similarity he shared with them. He was short and wiry, with a thin face that had been altered from its natural line by a broken nose. His mean eyes and the determined set of his sharp jawline suggested a man well able to defend himself against anybody who mistook his size as a sign of weakness. In contrast to the others, he wore a black shirt with a bootlace tie and a sheepskin jacket and his pants were levis with twin holsters tied down to his thighs. A matched pair of Colt revolvers fitted snugly into the holsters.

'They reckon as how it was an actor guy who done it,' Binns announced, gesturing pointedly with empty glass.

Elmer began to pour him a new drink.

'Fellow named Booth,' Carstairs augmented, savouring the taste of the whiskey.

Elmer stopped pouring. The man in the cape and the four at the poker table all stared at the Englishman in wide-eyed surprise.

'John Wilkes Booth shot the President?' the sullen-faced Elmer gasped.

'In the head,' Logan replied.

Carstairs nodded in confirmation, still the centre of attention. 'That's right, Elmer. He was seen. Escaped through a side door into an alley after firing a derringer at Mr Lincoln.'

The man in the cape sensed a pair of eyes burning into the side of his face and turned slowly to find the bartender staring at him with blatant distrust. He tried to ignore it, and lifted his glass.

'That's sure how it happened, Elmer,' Binns said into the still tense silence filling the bar. 'Rumour that there's a conspiracy to kill all the top men in the Government tonight. Host of Johnnie Rebs reckons as how Appomattox didn't finish the war – not really.'

Binns seemed about to continue, but caught sight of Elmer's suddenly venomous stare. His own eyes swivelled to discover the object of the barman's loathing and settled upon the smartly dressed old man. In their turn, Logan, Monahan and Carstairs became aware of the mounting unease in their midst and turned their heads to find the cause. Beyond the group at the bar counter, the other patrons felt the tension and craned their necks to see the old man's discomfort as the silence forced him to look up.

'Something you boys want?' he asked nervously, blinking as he surveyed the faces of the men around him.

The barman's suspicion had expanded into hatred. The others were confused as they alternated their attention between Elmer and the old man.

'You ever hear a man speak who sounded more Deep South than him, Bill?' Elmer asked, flicking his eyes momentarily towards Carstairs.

'Can't say that I have, Elmer,' the Englishman allowed, puzzled. 'Why do you ask, old son?'

'Ed talked about a conspiracy,' Elmer answered with heavy menace. 'Now, just a few minutes before Mr Lincoln got shot, John Wilkes Booth was in this very bar, drinking. Right alongside this here southerner.'

Confusion was replaced by intrigued interest on the faces of the watchers. The old man set down his glass on the bartop and a sudden spasm in his hand toppled it and set it rolling. The sound it made was like a rumble of thunder in the menacing stillness.

Carstairs reached out a well-manicured hand and caught the glass with cool ease as it dropped over the edge. The old man made a small move to push himself away from the bar, but the Englishman's voice halted him.

'What are you trying to tell us, Elmer?' he asked evenly, putting down the glass.

Elmer picked it up, dunked it in a pail of water beneath the bar and began to wipe it with a cloth. 'I'm telling it like it was,' he answered, refusing to unlock the stare fixed upon the old man's fear-clouded eyes. 'This here southerner suddenly goes outa his way to point out what time it is. Then Booth goes outa my place like he had a mighty important thing he had to do. But on the way, he kinda bumps into this here southerner – '

'I resent the implication of what you are – '

'Shut up, southerner,' Binns growled, stepping back and to the side.

This placed him immediately behind the old man, who had to grip the edge of the bartop to keep his mottled hands from trembling. There was a shuffling of boot leather each side of him as Logan and Monahan moved in close to him.

'Now, I couldn't see, because I'm one side of the bar and they're on the other,' Elmer continued. 'But maybe that bump wasn't accidental. Maybe this here southerner passed a derringer over to Booth.'

A rumble of angry conversation rose among the patrons seated at the tables. Panic sprang into the eyes of the old man and he shot fast glances to left and right, then over his shoulders. There were some twenty men in the barroom, and only one of these was looking at him with a degree of sympathy. He was a grizzled oldtimer with an untidy grey beard and watery blue eyes. The expressions of the others ranged from shocked surprise to glaring hatred.

'Gentlemen, please!' the man blurted out, his lower lip quivering.

'Sounds mighty suspicious to me, Bill,' Monahan said gruffly, his right hand folding around the butt of the Colt at his hip.

'Search him,' Carstairs instructed.

Sweat broke out on the old man's forehead and upper lip as Binns dropped into a crouch and ran his gnarled hands roughly over the expensive suiting, exploring every place where it would be possible to conceal a weapon.

'He ain't heeled, Bill,' he reported.

The drunk under the table began to snore again, after a period during which he had unaccountably been silent.

'Now that is suspicious,' Carstairs muttered thoughtfully, staring hard at the petrified old man. 'Southerner up here in Washington amongst all we northerners – and he doesn't have a gun.'

'I reckon he had one, but give it to Booth,' Elmer supplied.

'This is rid . . . ridiculous,' the old man stammered. 'I demand to – '

'You don't seem to be in a position to make any demands, old son,' Carstairs pointed out evenly.

Logan jerked at the crotch of his tight-fitting pants. 'Reckon Elmer's right, Bill,' he said. 'He musta passed his iron to Booth.'

'He helped to kill the President,' Binns put in with a note of awe in his voice.

'We ought to string him up,' Monahan growled.

The old man squeezed his eyes tight shut and the skin of his face was suddenly drained of colour. He seemed on the point of fainting. Monahan's comment was greeted with a moment of utter silence. Then the drunk dropped the empty bottle and as it thudded to the bare boards the sound signalled a menacing murmur of approval. A chair leg screeched against the floor as it was pushed back from a table.

'Hold on there, men.'

The almost physical pressure of concentration upon the caped man at the bar was lifted as all eyes swung towards the old timer, who had stood up.

'Is this southerner a friend of yours?' Carstairs asked with disdain.

Thc old timer refused to be provoked by the Englishman. 'No, he ain't,' he replied with soft-voiced slowness. 'But you got any complaint against him, you oughta tell the military or the police.'

'You sound like a sympathiser to me,' Carstairs accused.

The expressions of most of the men surrounding the old timer indicated they were prepared to agree with the Englishman's contention.

'For God's sake, he's right!' the old man exclaimed. 'I'm innocent and I can prove it. I was just here waiting for my – '

Monahan drew the revolver and jabbed it viciously into the old man's side. 'Shut your slobbering trap,' he rasped. 'I can't stand to hear that Southland talk of yours.'

The old timer took a step forward, towards the group at the

bar. 'This is Washington,' he blurted. 'You can't lynch a man here in the city. We got law and order here.'

'That how it was so easy to kill the President,' a man called derisively.

'You just can't do it, that's all,' the old timer insisted.

Carstairs' well-formed mouth took on a cruel set and his clear blue eyes clouded with anger. 'Jack?' he said softly.

'Yeah, Bill?' Logan replied.

'This insect is beginning to irritate me,' Carstairs told him, staring levelly at the the old timer.

'Swat it?' Logan asked, a quiet smile adding life to his unintelligent face.

'I'd like that.'

Logan was fat, but he was fast. One moment he was standing beside the caped man, absently tugging at his pants. Then he side stepped with incredible speed, his free hand streaking inside his jacket. Fear leapt across the features of the old timer as he turned to meet the attack. But his reflexes were far too slow. A foot-long wooden club with a two-inch diameter swung towards his head. It stung the tips of the fingers of his upraised hands and then landed with a sickening crack against his forehead. The ancient skin split open and thin blood squeezed out and flowed towards the closed eyes. The old timer crumpled to the floor with a sigh, his bloodied head thudding on to the highly polished toecap of Carstairs' right shoe.

The Englishman pulled back his foot and lashed out with a kick. It caught the unconscious man in the back of the neck and flipped him over on to his stomach. Blood dripped and was soaked up by the sawdust on the floor. The old timer breathed shallowly.

'Anyone else got any objections?' Logan asked, his eyes raking over the faces of the men as he hefted the club, as if testing its weight.

The inquiry was greeted with silence, except for the snores of the sleeping drunk.

'Good,' Logan said.

Carstairs nodded in satisfaction and fixed the old man with an evil stare. 'Make your peace,' he invited.

For long moments, the old man's anguish struck him dumb. Then, finally, he gasped: 'You're making a terrible mistake . . . '.

His voice trailed away as the strain became too much for his mind to bear. His legs buckled and his hands lost their strength, releasing the grip on the bartop. As he toppled backwards, Binns stepped out of the way and the unconscious form thudded heavily to the floor.

'Got a rope, Elmer?' Monahan asked.

Every man in the bar still in possession of his senses was caught in the grip of a high excitement as the bartender reached behind him and thudded a coil of rope on to the counter top.

'Lock the doors,' Carstairs ordered and a man stood up from a table to comply.

Monahan exhibited the strength in his wiry frame by stooping and hoisting the limp form of the old man with utter ease.

The drunk under the table spluttered to a degree of awareness and surveyed the scene before him with drink-blurred eyes. His alcohol-sodden brain could not reconcile the tableau with the surroundings in which he had passed out and accepted the images as part of a terrifying dream.

The old man in the cape was lifted on to a table and slapped into consciousness by Monahan as Binns formed one end of the rope into a noose. For a long time, the old man's brain was as befuddled as that of the drunk. He felt himself being forced to stand upright, then the constriction at his throat. He knew a man was holding him, but was not aware of another looping the free end of the rope over a ceiling beam and knotting it there. He saw a sea of faces in front and below him, but they were merely pale blobs against a blurred background and he was unable to discern their expressions.

Then, as the drunk sank back into his stupor, the old man's mind and vision cleared. And memory returned, filling him with trembling terror.

Monahan and Binns jumped to the floor. The men crowded in closer to the table on which the old man stood, their eyes bright with an almost sexual arousal of excitement. Terror rose into the old man's throat, swelling it against the fibrous harshness of the rope. His hands were free and he clawed at the noose, but there was no slack between the knot at the nape of his neck and the stout beam above him.

'You can't hang a man without a trial!' a voice called weakly.

The old man's distended eyes sought the source of the plea and focussed upon his sole ally, sprawled behind the crowd in a pool of his own blood.

Carstairs sighed and nodded curtly to the waiting Logan. The fat man approached the old timer, who had rolled on to his back and was starting to struggle into a sitting position. But when he saw Logan looming above him, he groaned and fell back, throwing up his hands to protect his bloodied face.

Logan grinned and changed his grip on the club, holding it like a dagger, pointing downwards. His arm swung and the flat end of the club's end thudded into the base of the old timer's stomach. The breath rushed out of the toothless mouth and the old timer jack-knifed his body, his hands streaking to clutch at the source of the new pain.

'Hush up,' Logan instructed softly.

Nobody witnessed the vicious assault, for attention was divided between the pathetically helpless form of the old man on the table, and the slim figure of Carstairs, who had stepped to the forefront of the watching group.

'He may have a point,' the Englishman allowed, stroking his clean-shaven chin reflectively as he surveyed the old man. 'So you may consider yourself on trial. The charge is conspiracy to assassinate the President of the United States. As a foreigner, I feel I am sufficiently unbiased to act as a fair judge. How do you plead, old son?'

The man on the table was still clutching at the noose, but he was unable to relieve the pressure on his windpipe. 'You can't – ' he croaked.

'He's guilty,' Binns said nonchalently, picking at his teeth with a filthy fingernail.

'Sure he's guilty,' Logan agreed, swinging the club before the pain-filled eyes of the old timer.

Monahan, resting a hand on each of his holstered guns, looked around the ring of eager-faced watchers, his menacing stare daring any man to complain against the arbitrary verdict. 'Guilty as all hell,' he muttered.

'A judge can't argue against that kind of unanimity,' Carstairs told the trembling old man, then stepped up closer to the table.

The drunk had ceased snoring again, but his heavy breathing reached stentorian pitch against the blanket of silence which descended over the barroom. Behind the bar, Elmer continued to wipe the glass of the condemned man, his hand movements increasing in speed as the moments were ticked away by the clock on the wall.

'Anything to say before I pass judgement?' Carstairs asked in a mock funereal tone.

The old man in the cape suddenly dropped his hands to his

sides, but not in dejection. The nightmare in which he had found himself was reaching a climax, and there would be no waking from it. He was going to die and nothing he could do or say would prevent his tormentors from completing the cruel act. Fear became a diamond-hard mass filling his stomach, but it withdrew the physical manifestations of the emotion. He stood stiffly to his full height and his features grew calm. His stance and his expression were composed and dignified.

'May you all rot in hell,' he whispered.

'May you welcome us there, old son,' Carstairs said. 'Judgement of this court is . . . '. He raised his right leg, then thrust it forward. The table tilted and toppled. Gasps ripped from the throats of the spectators in a single sound as if from one man. The old man's high-buttoned boots slid off the canting surface and there was a sharp crack as his neck was broken. His body swung gently in mid-air above the overturned table.

Carstairs looked around the faces of the men, many of them betraying the shock of remorse in the knowledge that the senseless act was done and could not be undone. A few turned away from the gruesome sight of the hanging man. The Englishman reached behind him and pushed against the dangling legs of the dead man, setting the body swinging at a faster rate. A personable grin spread across the young man's handsome features as he completed the phrase he had started: ' . . . a suspended sentence.'

CHAPTER THREE

ADAM Steele reined his bay gelding to a halt at the crest of a rise and split his mouth in a gentle smile as he surveyed the lights of the city spread before him. It had been a long ride from Richmond and he spent a few relaxed moments in quiet contemplation of the end of the journey. Then he sighed and heeled the horse forward down the gentle incline towards a turnpike which led into Washington.

He rode upright, but not tall in the Western saddle. He was just a shade over five feet six inches in height, his build compact rather than slight, and suggested adequate strength instead of great power. Like so many young men who had survived the bitter fighting of the war just ended, he looked older than his actual years, which totalled twenty-eight. He had a long face with regular features which gave him a nondescript handsomeness: likely to interest women though certainly not sweep them off their feet. His mouthline was gentle, his nose straight and his black eyes honest. His hair was pre-naturally grey with only a few hanks of dark red to show its former colouration. It was trimmed neat and short and this was the only obvious sign of the five years he had spent in the army of the Confederate States. A more subtle indication of how he had used the war years could be seen in his clothes. Black riding boots; dark grey pants, oddly slit at the seam about the calf of the right leg; a white shirt with a neckerchief decorated by an ornate pin; a hip-length sheepskin coat in dark brown; a low-crown black hat and black leather gloves. All were brand new, with the store stiffness still in the material – purchased immediately upon his discharge to replace the grey uniform of a cavalry lieutenant. All over the country, tailors were growing rich supplying new clothes to men anxious to shed uniform serge.

The city was very quiet as Steele entered the streets of its southern section and he was mildly surprised at this. Washington was the capital of the victorious northern states and he had expected it still to be in the throes of triumphant revelry even this long after Lee's surrender.

But he did not give too much thought to the matter, beyond appreciating that he was spared the expected humiliation of seeing his former enemies rejoicing in the defeat of the Cause. For he had another, more important subject on his mind. And it was this upon which he ruminated as he rode the gelding along the silent meagrely lit streets of Washington.

He had no trouble finding his way to his destination, for he had been a frequent visitor to the city in pre-war days and little had changed during the intervening years. So it was not until he turned on to Tenth Street that he pulled up short in surprise.

The street was as quiet as all the others had been, but there was a difference. Where the others had been deserted, this one was crowded with people. The great majority of them were huddled together in a large group before a house diagonally across the street from the darkened façade of Ford's Theatre. Most of the buildings lining the street were in darkness and this seemed to emphasise the wedges of light falling from the house which held the crowd's interest. In the splashes of yellow, the faces of the people were wan and sad. The rifle barrels of the soldiers ranged in front of the house, keeping the crowd well back, gleamed with an oily sheen.

Occasionally, one or more of the silent spectators would drift away from the crowd. One such was an old woman who stepped unwittingly in front of Steele's horse as he urged the animal forward. She looked up at the rider, showing no emotion at almost being trampled. Deep shock dwelled behind her moist eyes.

'What's happening here, ma'am?' Steele asked, his voice smoothed by a Virginia drawl, as he touched his hat brim with a gloved hand.

The old woman blinked, and a tear was squeezed from the corner of each eye. 'Mr Lincoln,' she replied tremulously. 'They've shot Mr Lincoln.'

Under different circumstances, Steele knew he might have felt a surge of joy and expectation that the event could signal new hope for the South to rise against defeat. But he had come to Washington determined to forget the past and adjust himself to the best future he could make.

Even so, he had difficulty in injecting a degree of the mournful into his voice as he asked: 'Is the President dead?'

The old woman shook her head as she turned away to go around behind Steele's horse. 'But he's dying. Won't last out the night, they say.'

Steele took a final look down the street towards the house and the melancholy crowd before it, then jerked over the reins to angle his horse towards Elmer's Barroom. It was not in complete darkness, for a dim light flickered far in back of one of the windows. After he had looped the reins over the hitching rail at the edge of the sidewalk, he approached the doors and they swung open in front of him.

'We're closed, mister,' Elmer announced as the newcomer crossed the threshold. 'Mark of respect for the President.'

The doors squeaked closed behind Steele and he halted abruptly. He saw Elmer standing behind the bar, using the turned down light of a single kerosene lamp to count the night's takings. He could hear one man snoring and another groaning, but they were beyond the reach of the flickering light. He could smell stale cigar smoke and spilled whiskey. He could sense death.

'I just heard,' he said, moving forward towards the bar, feeling the sawdust beneath the soles of his new boots. 'After getting news like that, a man needs a drink. Whiskey.'

He pulled up short again, as something brushed against his shoulder. His pupils had distended to the low level of light now and as he looked up, he could discern the limply hanging form of the dead man. The body revolved slowly from where he had collided with a dangling leg.

'Turn up the lamp, bartender,' he said softly.

Elmer continued to chink loose change, taking it from his apron pocket and stacking it on the bartop. 'Told you, mister, the place is closed up for the night,' he growled.

The sleeping drunk stopped snoring and smacked his lips as if his imagination was enjoying a good meal.

'The view's lousy anyway,' the old timer rasped, crawling towards the bar and using the rail to push himself on to all fours.

'You don't turn up that lamp, I'll kill you,' Steele said, his drawling voice still pitched low. But it was high on menace.

Elmer's head snapped up and he peered intently through the darkness towards the newcomer. His face in the lamp light was made uglier by a scowl. He could not see Steele clearly and it was for this reason he reached out and turned up the wick. His free hand dragged a Manhattan Navy Model out from beneath the bar. When the pool of light had spread far enough to illuminate Steele and the hanging man, the revolver was cocked and aimed.

'You don't look capable, mister,' Elmer said, noting that Steele wore no gunbelt and his hands were empty.

Steele was staring up at the swollen face of the old man. His own features were empty of expression and when he turned to look at Elmer and started to walk towards him he still gave no outward sign of what he was thinking.

'What happened here?' he asked, the threat missing from his low tones. But neither was he concerned with the pointing gun in the bartender's hand. He glanced casually to his right and saw the bearded old timer with the bloody forehead climbing painfully to his feet. Then to the left, where the sleeping drunk was just a lumpy shadow against the deeper shadow beneath the table.

Elmer's sullen eyes met Steele's open stare, then took in at close range the man's easy-going features and unprovoking build. He lumped this all together with the lack of visible weapons and decided his unwanted customer had a tough mouth but nothing with which to back it up. He put the gun down beneath the bar and started to dig for more coins.

'A guy blasted the President over at the theatre,' he rasped. 'Got clean away.' He nodded towards the man hanging from the beam. 'That guy passed the gun to the murderer. Didn't have the sense to take it on the lam.' A sour grin glowed in his eyes and twisted his mouth. 'Me and a few others kinda forced him to hang around.'

The old timer was leaning his elbows on the bar, nursing his broken head in the palms of his hands. 'Weren't no proof of that!' he snapped, without looking up. 'Ed Binns and his pals just up and hanged the old man on account of what you told 'em.'

Elmer glowered hatefully at the old timer. 'He give the gun to Booth, I'm telling you,' he snarled.

'And you can give me a drink,' Steele said.

Elmer sighed, seemed about to refuse, then swung around and swept a shot glass and bottle from the shelf behind him. He set the glass on the bartop and poured the right measure without looking. Steele proffered no money, and neither did he reach for the drink.

'What if you were wrong?' he asked.

Elmer banged the bottle down angrily. 'Just drink your drink and get out so I can close up,' he snarled. 'I weren't wrong.'

'You were wrong,' Steele said.

With his left hand, Steele tugged at his ear lobe. His right hand came fast out of the pocket on that side of his jacket and Elmer's eyes widened with terror as he saw the tiny two-shot derringer clutched in the fist. The gun went off with a small crack. The shattered whiskey bottle made a louder noise. Elmer fell backwards, crashing against the display shelf. His hands clutched at his bulbous stomach. Small shards of broken glass glittered against the dark stains of whiskey covering his apron. He looked down at himself and gasped when he saw the blood oozing between his fingers.

The old timer forgot his own pain as he savoured the agony of Elmer.

'His name was Benjamin Steele. And my name is Adam Steele.' the man said softly. 'That was my father you killed.'

The pain had had time to reach Elmer now, and it overflowed his eyes in the form of tears as he brought his head up to look at the man he had so badly misjudged. Steele held the shocked stare of the other, as he slid the derringer back in his pocket and used his left hand to draw out a match. He struck it on his thumbnail and in the sudden flare of yellow light his eyes seemed not to be as one with the rest of his features. For the lines of his face had a composed, innocuous set – while the eyes, pulled wide, blazed with a seemingly unquenchable fury.

Then the flaring match was arced forward. Elmer emitted a strangled sob of horror, throwing up his hands. The match sailed between them and bounced against his chest. It fell to the floor, but not before a fragile flame licked up from the whiskey-sodden material of his shirt. He beat at it with a blood-stained hand, the motion fanning the fire. Within a terrifying few seconds, as the fury died within Steele, the bartender's massive body was enveloped in searing flames. As shreads of charred clothing fell from him and the intense heat swept over his naked skin, his sobs became strangled cries, pitched so high they sounded almost feminine. He threw himself to the floor and began to roll backwards and forward as he beat at hungry flames. But the whiskey-soaked sawdust behind the bar counter only added fuel to the agonising fire.

The old timer's horror at the lynching was as nothing compared to the revulsion he felt as he watched Elmer's pitifully ineffectual attempts to beat out the flames. But he made no attempt to intervene, conscious of the evil lurking beneath the deceptively gentle surface of the young man standing beside him.

'Innocent man getting lynched,' Steele said, still softly. 'Fair burns a man up, doesn't it?'

The old timer was at last able to tear his gaze away from the weakening struggle of the human torch. But he discovered that Steele had not been addressing him. Instead, the blank-faced young man had muttered the comment to himself as he turned and moved towards the limp form of his father. He set the table upright and the lifeless body took on a curved posture as the high buttoned boots rested on the top. Steele leaned to the right, bending his leg so that the slit in the seam of his pants gaped open. His hand reached inside and drew from his boot a wooden-handled knife with a six inch blade. There was not a single sign of grief in his expression or his actions as he climbed on to the table. The finely-honed blade of the knife sliced through the hanging rope in a matter of moments. He pulled the noose from around the neck to reveal an ugly red weal in the dead skin. After sliding the knife back into the sheath strapped to his boot, he lifted the slight form of his father in both arms and stepped down from the table. His empty eyes surveyed the old timer across half the width of the barroom.

'You mentioned a name?' he said softly.

The old timer swallowed hard and glanced over the bartop. The charred body of Elmer was still. The smell of him masked the more familiar odours of the room. A wide area of sawdust was smouldering, only needing a draught to explode into renewed fire.

'Sure, Mr Steele,' he said hoarsely. 'Ed Binns. There was a feller name of Logan with them. And I heard Elmer call anothr guy Carstairs. He was a foreigner. Talked English, but not like an American.'

The weight of the body was no strain to Steele. 'Know where I'll find them?' he asked.

The old timer shook his head. Then said hurriedly: 'I used to know Ed Binns' old man. Had a drapery store out in Foothills, Tennessee. Ed always was the wild one: even when he was a young shaver, Mr Steele. Bigger he got, worser he got.'

'He's got as big as he's going to get,' Steele said. 'Grateful to you.'

He turned and walked towards the door, carrying the body of

his father as if it weighed no more than a baby. When he pushed out through the doors, frosty night air wafted in and a heap of sawdust exploded into fire with a dull plop.

'It's disgusting,' a woman said shrilly as the swing doors squeaked closed. 'The President dying and men get falling down drunk.'

The old timer cast a fearful glance at the spreading carpet of fire behind the bar counter and staggered across to the man sleeping beneath the table. Hoofbeats sounded out on the street as he prodded the sleeping form with his boot. The man grunted and snapped open his eyes.

'Come on, Henry,' the old timer said urgently. 'Let's go home. Elmer won't be serving no more drinks.'

CHAPTER FOUR

MIDNIGHT was long gone when Lieutenant George C. Carey rapped his knuckles on the door marked GENERAL MILTON K. DEAN – CHIEF OF MILITARY INTELLIGENCE.

'Come in!' the general said curtly and Carey complied, entering a large office with panelled walls and a floor covered with a deep-pile carpet. It was lit meagrely with a single oil lamp on one corner of a large desk. The desk top was littered with sheaves of papers, several unfolded maps, a photograph of the general's wife and another of President Lincoln: the latter not yet draped by the black ribbon which was visible beneath the glass paperweight.

The general, tall and thin, his head bald and the face beneath hung with slack, wrinkled skin, was just sitting down behind the desk as Carey closed the door reverently behind him and saluted.

'Your men are ready, Lieutenant?' Dean demanded, touching his deeply scored forehead and then waving the junior officer into the chair before the desk.

'Yes, sir,' Carey replied brightly. 'And anxious to leave.' He injected a mournful note into his voice. 'Is there any further news from the Peterson House, sir?'

Carey was twenty-five and a war veteran. He had done a great deal of front line fighting in sixty-one and two before being wounded at Antietam Creek. Then he had been assigned to an army post in Indian Territory which was supposed to have been an easy number. And so it could have been, for a man willing to turn a blind eye towards his superiors' trafficking in arms for the Confederacy. The efficient manner in which Carey dealt with the situation at the fort, severing a vital supply line for the Rebels, resulted in re-assignment to Army Intelligence in Washington. Here, he served with as much distinction as elsewhere.

It was because of this excellent record that Dean had selected the young junior officer for such an important duty.

'President Lincoln is deteriorating fast,' the general said with a sigh, rubbing his weary eyes. 'There is little hope. But the doctors think the Secretary of State will survive.'

Carey's lanky body stiffened in the chair and his good-looking face revealed deep shock. 'Mr Seward was shot, too?'

The general shook his head. 'Stabbed. With members of his family at home.' He fixed the young man with a level stare. 'And there's more, lieutenant. We have information that there was also a plan to assassinate Vice-President Johnson.'

'My God!' Carey exclaimed. 'Mass murder. They're madmen!'

'Unreasoning men with an unreasonable motive,' Dean corrected. 'Dedicated to the overthrow by force of the duly elected Government of the United States.'

'Confederates, sir?'

Beyond the confines of the dimly lit office, the city was quiet. Inside the panelled walls the silence was funereal in its heaviness. The general's chair creaked as he stretched out his legs, seeking to relieve the muscle ache.

'We know that many thousands – maybe millions – of supporters of the Southern Cause are disenchanted with the outcome of the war, lieutenant,' he said. 'It was to be expected that anti-Union feelings would run high. But the tragic events of this night do not comprise a mere impulsive backlash against defeat.'

Carey leaned forward in his chair, aware that General Dean was reaching his point. All Carey knew so far was that he had been ordered to prepare a cavalry troop to combat readiness. He had surmised that he and the men were required to perform some duty in connection with the crime committed at Ford's Theatre.

'The violence in Washington is part of a well-organised plot,' the fatigued general went on. 'Your troop is just one unit of law-enforcement being deployed to track down the plotters and bring them to justice.'

Dean levered himself up and began to pace the room.

'But naturally,' he said to the eager-faced lieutenant. 'Army intelligence desires to have the honour of capturing these men.' He altered the direction of his pacing and halted at the side of Carey's chair. His face as he looked down at the younger man was momentarily lit by the fire within him. 'I don't merely desire it,

Lieutenant Carey. I demand it!'

Carey nodded enthusiastically. 'You can depend on me, sir.'

For a long moment, Dean was not entirely convinced. Carey was not much more than a boy, fresh-faced and innocent looking, as if he still had at least one hand firmly clutched to his mother's apron strings. But then the general remembered the young man's record and he returned to his chair and sat down with a sigh. His own record was far better, mainly because he had lived longer and been a soldier for more years than he cared to remember. That was the trouble. His record was a matter of history and the long years of making it had drained him of the energy to match his spirit. Now the army was filled with young men like Carey, literally fresh from the war: able to put into physical action the schemes and plans which wearied soldiers of Dean's generation had to work out.

'Very well,' he said, closing his eyes and massaging the lids with his thumbs. 'Those are your orders – to track down the plotters. We have only one lead. This afternoon, an Englishman and three Americans were seen in the company of Booth. These same four were at the theatre tonight and left immediately the shot was fired. They entered a drinking establishment across Tenth Street and there lynched an innocent man after accusing him of complicity with Booth.'

'To try to divert suspicion away from themselves, sir?' Carey suggested.

'Perhaps,' Dean said reflectively, and made a motion with his hand to indicate the briefing was ended. 'The four are front line activists, lieutenant,' Dean went on as Carey rose from the chair before the desk. 'Remember, it's the men directing them we want.'

'Sir!' Carey acknowledged, slapping up another smart salute, and getting a weary response from the general.

'You might as well know it,' the senior officer said suddenly as Carey reached the door, and waited for the lieutenant to turn to face him. 'They might have murdered the man at the bar because they knew who he was.'

'Sir?'

'Ben Steele,' Dean supplied. 'Unlikely you'd come across the name. He was a personal friend of President Lincoln. He was also a good friend to this department of the army and the Union army in general. One of the best agents we had.'

CHAPTER FIVE

ADAM Steele had never before cried as a man, and he considered he achieved adulthood at the age of twelve. But he wept a great deal on the trip south from Washington. For most of the way it was night and there was no one to see him. Then, when dawn broke, his emotions were exhausted, squeezed dry of the capacity to feel grief or express it. Those early risers who saw the lone rider on the bay gelding, travelling with a body slumped across the horse in front of the saddle, veered away from him. For there was something in his upright posture, the set of his head and his unwavering stare to the front which warned against physical approach or even a verbal greeting.

He still had more than two miles to go when he caught sight of all that remained of his former home. Shafts of bright sunlight angling in low from the east pierced cruelly into the blackened ruin of the plantation house. The west wall still stood, more or less intact. And the stoop at the front was still there, littered with fallen masonry from the upper floors. But apart from this, the house was now no more than a pile of sooted stone and charred wood. And the vast fields around it, once the colour of good Virginia soil or the seasonal hue of strong-growing tobacco, were now a single expanse of ebon and grey.

As the gelding crossed the northern boundary of the property, his hooves erupted small puffs of grey ash and black soot: the dry and useless residue of an act of mass hatred.

Steele noted fresh tracks in the fire dust, showing that a single rider had headed towards the ruined house not long ago. And if he had left, it had not been by the same trail he had arrived. Then, as Steele drew closer to the house, he saw a saddled horse hitched to one of several half burned upright posts which had formerly supported the stoop's wooden canopy. And a regular creaking sound drew his attention to a figure in a rocking chair further along the stoop. He recognised the lanky frame and lean features of Jim Bishop.

As Steele reined his horse to a stop at the foot of the steps which used to lead up to the front door, the man who had been born on the same day as himself and who had been his friend since childhood, slowly stood up. Sunlight glinted on the deputy sheriff's badge pinned to his shirt front. The garish shine emphasised the mournful dullness in his eyes.

'I heard they hung your dad, Adam,' Bishop said sadly.

He wore a revolver at each hip. His clothes were well-worn, but clean and neatly pressed. His pleasant face was clean shaven and only slightly dust marked by the ride from town. By contrast, Steele's appearance showed many signs of his long trip. His new clothes were dusty and creased and his jaw and cheeks were heavily matted with prickly bristles.

He nodded and then slid from the saddle and turned his back on the deputy as he unfastened the rope which held the body in place.

'You heard why, Bish?' he asked.

Bishop stayed at the top of the steps, squinting into the rising sun. 'The telegraph said they accused him of being part of the plot.'

Steele interrupted his work on the knots for a moment, to stare out over the blackened fields. Then he went to work again. 'You know how wrong they were.'

Bishop's nod was unseen by his life-long friend. 'Sure, Adam. If it was you they said was in on the plot, I'd maybe have to consider it could be true. But your dad and Mr Lincoln were – '

'I was on the losing side, Bish,' Steele put in evenly. 'I fought for the South and we lost. But we lost honourably.'

He released the final knot and eased his father's body gently down into his arms. The cape had hung over the bloated features during the ride, and he left it thus now as he turned to survey Bishop and the ruin behind the lawman.

'Some ain't so ready to forget and forgive so easy, Adam,' Bishop said with a sigh. 'When word got out your dad was working as an agent for the Federal Government, there was no stopping folk coming out here to do all this.'

He raised a hand and gestured to encompass the entire scene of destruction.

'We'd have built it again,' Steele murmured. 'When I was told what happened here, I had to try to heal the old rift with him. He wanted it that way, too. That's why we agreed to meet in Washington. We'd have forgotten the war.'

'Some things just ain't meant to be, Adam,' Bishop replied softly, dropping his hand so that both were hanging close to his gun butts. 'You shouldn't have killed that bar-tender. They telegraphed me to take you in if you showed up. I figured you'd bring him home.'

'You intend to do it, Bish?' Steele asked, without provocation in either voice or gesture.

'You know my feeling for the law,' the deputy answered. 'It's more important than friendship. But I don't feel too bad about putting you under arrest, Adam. You'll get acquitted, sure as the sun comes up every morning.'

Steele responded to the comment with a slight nod, then turned away. 'Before I do anything else, Bish, I have to bury him.'

Bishop started down the steps. 'Sure, Adam, you got to do that,' he agreed.

Steele led the way around the massive heap of burned out rubble and then angled away, towards the charred stump of what had once been a thousand-year-old shade oak tree. There was a mound close by, which had once been covered by close-clipped grass. Now it was just a hump of blackened earth. The picket fence around it and the cross which had marked it had been reduced to ashes. A spade, the handle charred but still serviceable, leaned against the tree stump.

Steele set down the body gently and eyed Bishop, who shrugged, somewhat embarrassed.

'Like I said, I figured you'd bring him home to bury him. I'd have started, but I thought you might have a special place in mind.'

Steele crossed and picked up the shovel. 'I'm grateful to you, Bish,' he said. 'Alongside Ma would be right, wouldn't it?'

'I reckon,' Bishop said.

Steele struck the ground hard with the spade and the powdery embers rose to release an acrid odour. But soon he had cut out a shallow trench and the clean smell of good earth was rising from the fresh grave. He worked hard and without rest until Bishop stepped forward and took the spade from his gloved hands. But the deputy was not allowed to continue for long before Steele reached out mutely for the tool.

There was only one short exchange of words, and that as the sweating Steele ceased digging and looked up from the grave which was almost as deep as he was tall.

'Down enough, you think?'

'I reckon,' Bishop replied, squinting into the sun, which had risen well clear of the horizon, growing brighter and hotter by the minute. 'Want me to hand him down?'

'I'd be grateful,' Steele replied.

Bishop wondered momentarily if he should have offered to try to make up a coffin from burned house timber while Steele was digging. But it was too late now. He lowered the stiff body of the old man down into the arms of Steele and the son arranged his father reverently on the bare earth. He had to use a great deal of strength to bend the arms at the elbows so that the dead man's hands formed a cross on his chest.

Then Steele gripped Bishop's extended hand and hoisted himself out of the grave. He avoided looking down into the trench until the body was completely covered by soil. Then he worked furiously to shovel the remainder of the earth into the grave, and formed a small mound on top with that which had been displaced by the body. He neither asked for nor seemed to expect help in the easier work of filling in.

'You want to put some kind of marker on him, Adam?' the young lawman asked as Steele hurled away the spade and surveyed the result of his labour.

'You think they'd leave it in place?' Steele asked.

'Guess not,' Bishop replied sadly.

'But I'll say a prayer for him,' Steele said.

Bishop nodded and took off his hat as he moved to the other side of the grave. Steele kept his on as he sank to his knees beside the low pile of fresh earth. He searched for something in his pockets, seemed not to find it and then bowed his head over clasped hands. His lips moved, but no sound emerged. For some time he kept his eyes tight closed, but then he cracked them to maintain a furtive watch on his childhood friend.

Bishop saw the shimmer of sunlight on tears through the cracked lids and sensed a sudden tension in Steele's kneeling body. He let go of his hat with one hand and splayed his fingers towards the butt of the Colt on his right hip.

'Don't try it, Bish,' Steele warned coldly.

His left hand remained in an attitude of prayer. His right swivelled forward and became formed into a fist, fingers curled around the butt and trigger of the derringer.

'I've got my duty to perform, Adam!' Bishop rasped angrily, hurt rather than frightened.

Steele nodded. 'So have I,' he replied, easing to his feet, ever watchful of the man on the other side of the mound. 'One down and four to go. Don't make me make it five.'

Bishop tried to sound nonchalent, but kept his hand well clear of his gun. 'You won't kill me, Adam. We been friends since we swum in the creek together before we could walk.'

'You know what they say about blood being thicker than water, Bish. It goes even for old blood and old water.'

Bishop put on his hat and a mixture of resignation and sadness showed on his open face. 'You light out, Adam, I'll catch up with you,' he said.

'I guess we're both experienced grave-diggers, Bish,' Steele allowed. 'But one a day is enough for any man. Drop the gunbelt. Another time and another place, uh?'

The deputy's movements were slow and careful as he unbuckled his belt and allowed it to drop heavily to the ground. 'Any time, any place,' he promised.

'Round to the front,' Steele instructed, motioning with the gun for Bishop to lead the way back to the stoop.

The sun was nearing its noon peak and was very hot as Steele finished tying Bishop to the rocker, using the rope which had held his father's body on the gelding. He hooked the deputy's gunbelt over a charred upright. Then the two men surveyed each other with an almost complete lack of emotion: but in each pair of eyes there was room for a small degree of remorse.

'Wasn't much saved, Adam,' Bishop said, breaking the long silence which had held since the last word spoken at the graveside. 'But I found something while I was poking around – waiting for you.'

Steele looked at him quizzically and saw him nod towards one end of the stoop. He moved slowly in the direction indicated and stopped short when he saw the rifle resting against a piece of fallen masonry. He looked back towards the figure bound to the chair.

'Guess your dad was proud of it,' Bishop called. 'You might not be.'

Steele picked it up. It was an unusual weapon – a Colt Hartford sporting model: a six-shot revolving percussion rifle, .44 calibre. The barrel was covered with soot and the rosewood stock was slightly charred, but the action worked smoothly. It was fully loaded. As Steele ran a gloved hand over the stock, he wiped soot from a narrow gold plate screwed to the wood. The inscription was in a flowing script: To BENJAMIN P. STEELE, WITH GRATITUDE – ABRAHAM LINCOLN.

'Thanks,' Steele said as he turned and strode towards his horse. He slid the rifle into the boot. 'It's a nice gun, no matter who bought it.'

He swung up into the saddle.

Bishop squinted into the sun. 'I could die out here like this.'

'I'll shoot you if you like, Bish,' Steele offered. 'But I haven't got the time to bury you.'

The deputy stared hard at the impassive sweat and dirt streaked face of the man on the horse and realised he meant what he said. He swallowed hard. 'I'll take my chances.'

Steele nodded. 'Where there's life, there's hope, uh?'

'For me Adam,' Bishop replied sourly. 'But not for you. I got my orders to bring you in. And I aim to carry them out. The law's the law. You're making a mistake, Adam. As bad as the men who lynched your dad. Law's got to be carried out by duly-elected officers else it ain't no law at all.'

Steele didn't seem to be listening to Bishop. 'I'm grateful for the gun,' he said as he kneed his horse away from the stoop, facing him towards the south-west.

'No matter where you go, I'll be in back of you,' Bishop promised.

Steele nodded. 'That's good, Bish,' he said softly. 'When a man's got troubles, he needs a friend to stick by him.'

Bishop's expression showed hate and his voice quivered with soft venom. 'Our friendship ended when you pulled that gun on me.'

Again, Steele was not listening. He heeled the gelding into a walk, then into a canter. He looked back only once, and this towards the two graves, one old and one new. Soot and dust billowed higher as he drove the horse into a full gallop across the burned-out fields of the plantation.

Bishop craned his neck and watched the rider until he was out of sight, the clearly-marked tracks pointing out the direction of his flight with the clarity of marker arrows. Then the deputy glanced sourly at the broiling sun before staring into the heat shimmer behind which lay town. Sweat beads oozed from his pores and he wondered how long the sheriff would wait before sending out to see what had happened to him.

CHAPTER SIX

IT was mid-afternoon before Bishop's eyes stinging with the squeezed-out sweat of his own body, discerned a fast-riding horseman racing through the haze towards the ruined house. As he crossed the property boundary, he veered his mount to one side to follow exactly the line of approach adopted by Steele. More charred remains from the fire were puffed up by thudding hooves.

Bishop waited with mounting anticipation for the newcomer to draw near and relieve his sweating discomfort. But when the rider halted his horse before the stoop, the deputy experienced a pang of apprehension. He was not from the law office, nor even from town. And he was the kind of stranger in the kind of mood to make Bishop hate Steele with a greater intensity for rendering him helpless.

'He's been and he's gone, right?' the man asked, eyeing Bishop's predicament with scornful disdain.

He was a big man of about fifty. He had a mean, cruel-mouthed, hard-eyed face that was very pale against his black frock coat and black derby hat. The coat was open to show a revolver in a holster hanging from the front of his belt, butt turned towards his left.

The young deputy struggled against revealing his nervousness to the still mounted man. 'Who's asking?'

'Lovell, Washington Police Department.'

The sudden smile that decorated the deputy's face was a sign of how much strain Lovell's menacing appearance had placed on him. As the city policeman swung down from the saddle, he jerked a leather billfold from his shirt pocket and waved it negligently, showing a silver star.

'You're Deputy Bishop,' he said, coming up the steps. I talked to the sheriff in town. Told me you came out to get Steele.'

Lovell's voice and expression spoke volumes for his low regard of the country lawman. Then he pivoted slowly, surveying the scene of destruction from close range. A slight upturning of the corners of his mouth indicated his enjoyment of what he saw.

'No pa and no home,' he murmured. 'He must be feeling real mean about now.'

Bishop looked down at the ropes binding him to the rocker. 'I was Adam Steele's best friend,' he said, his tone a mixture of misery and hate.

'Glad you said *was*,' Lovell replied, returning his scornful attention to Bishop. 'I'm his worst enemy.'

Bishop squinted up at him. 'I guess you're here on official business, Mr Lovell?'

Lovell put a hand under his coat, as if he intended to scratch his armpit. But it came away fast, clutching a knife. Bishop had come to realise that the mean look in the man's eyes was a permanent fixture, but he still could not control a shiver. It chilled the sweat on his body and set the chair rocking back and forth. The Washington policeman tested the sharpness of the knife against the ball of his thumb.

'Official, deputy,' he confirmed, stepping up close to the swaying rocker. 'Steele killed a man in cold blood inside city limits. Police Department takes an official view of that.'

He twisted his wrist so that the knife was pointed towards Bishop. The deputy rocked back. His eyes grew wide and his mouth gaped open. He rocked forward, stare locked on the mean eyes of Lovell. The knife point pinged against the badge on the deputy's chest. Bishop stopped rocking. A sigh rasped from his dry throat as Lovell laughed and began to saw through the ropes.

'Of course, we lawmen are human,' he said easily. 'Even on official business, we got our personal feelings. And when a man comes to the law after being a bounty hunter, it's hard to lose some of the old habits. Bringing them in dead is easier than the other way.'

The final bond was severed and as Lovell stepped back, Bishop moved quickly from the chair. He spent only a few moments in flexing stiffened muscles, then reached for the hanging gunbelt and buckled it on. He immediately felt better. More so when

Lovell had replaced the knife in its shoulder sheath.

'But with Adam Steele, it won't be just habit, uh?' Bishop asked.

Lovell's eyes came up and locked on the other man's face again. 'I told you, deputy. I got personal feelings about him.'

'What – '

'Personal and private!' Lovell barked.

He continued to out-stare the other man for a moment, then whirled and went down the steps. He hoisted himself smoothly into the saddle, exhibiting his familiarity with horses.

'I've got my orders, same as you,' Bishop said sharply.

Lovell showed his parody of a smile. 'But I talked to a guy who knows where Steele is headed. I only swung down this way because I figured he'd bury his pa first.'

Bishop was good with a gun, his left hand only fractionally slower than the right. Armed with the Colts he feared no man. He showed his confidence now, as he descended from the stoop and halted less than three feet from the man who sat with such quiet menace in the saddle.

'I can ride with you, or behind you,' Bishop said. 'No man gets away with what he did to me. Especially not a friend.'

Lovell looked disdainfully down at Bishop, unprovoked by the young deputy's self-assurance. '*Was* a friend,' he reminded.

Bishop nodded. 'Right.'

'Personal with you, too?'

'Right again.'

Lovell pondered a moment, then shrugged. 'Something else I learned when I was bounty hunting in the south-west. Two against one is better odds than even steven.'

'I'll get my horse,' Bishop said hurriedly. 'It's out back.'

He started to turn away, but Lovell's threatening voice halted him.

'One thing?'

'What's that?'

Lovell's voice was as cold as his eyes. 'I never split rewards.'

Bishop was puzzled. 'There's no bounty on Adam.'

Lovell raised a hand and pointed his index finger to touch his forehead and heart. 'Not in dollars,' he said softly. 'But here and here is where I'll enjoy my reward. And seeing Steele dead won't be enough. It'll have to be me that kills him.'

Bishop frowned, then nodded. 'All right, Lovell. What he did to you must have been worse than the trick he pulled on me. I'll be happy just seeing him get what he deserves.'

Lovell touched his hat brim in acknowledgement, then watched Bishop go from sight around the blackened ruin of the house. He waited only a moment before clucking to his horse and wheeling it. He held the animal to a walk as he picked up the tracks left by Steele's gelding and started out across the parched fields. He didn't turn around as he heard Bishop cantering to catch up with him.

'He's got better than three hours start,' the deputy said as he drew level with the city policeman.

'So let's do some whittling!' Lovell yelled, and thudded his heels hard against the flanks of his horse.

A black cloud billowed out behind the galloping riders.

CHAPTER SEVEN

AN evening quiet hung lethargically over the single street of Foothills, disturbed only by the shuffling gaits and low-voiced conversations of a few strollers. It had been a hot day and most of the hard-working citizens were too tired for riotous activities. Not that there was much opportunity in this community for any but the simplest pleasures. Most of the frame buildings lining the street were private dwellings, but there was a business section at the centre of town, flanking a small plaza. Here was the bank, a saloon, a livery stable and blacksmithy, a few shops supplying essentials, a church and the Foothills Hotel. It was the only part of town which boasted sidewalks and on the raised planking before the hotel was a living tableau advertising the town's main pleasure. Lounging in weathered chairs dragged from the lobby was an overweight and overpainted woman in her fifties and three young whores. They fanned themselves wearily with cheaply ornate fans and eyed the strollers with bored and scornful stares. For most of the citizens taking the evening air were either women or men escorting women. The few lone men who did enter the plaza always headed for the saloon, showing their preference for a cool beer rather than a professionally warm woman.

But suddenly the heavy-jowled face of the madam broke into a smile and she eased her ample frame up from the chair. The girls, and several of the people on the plaza heard the same sound which had attracted her attention, and turned to look towards the east. The hoofbeats of many horses grew in volume and after a few moments a troop of cavalrymen came into sight at the side of a hillock.

The madam broadened her smile as she swung around to look at the girls. 'Action stations, ladies,' she said. 'Prepare to surrender to boarders.'

Riding at the head of his troop, Lieutenant Carey glanced gratefully at the town marker and slowed the pace to a walk as he moved between the silent façades of the first houses on the street. There were twenty men at his back, dusty and saddle sore as they rode in ranks of two formation. Eighteen were enlisted troopers, besides a sergeant and a corporal. All were just as happy to see the town marker as was the officer. And eyed the women outside the hotel with an equal amount of interest. Not a single man in the detachment noticed the sign BINNS' DRAPERY above the store next door to the livery on the opposite side of the plaza.

'Halt them, but keep them mounted, sergeant,' Carey instructed as the head of the column drew level with the hotel entrance with its blatent display of goods for sale.

'Troooop, haaaalt!' the fat faced sergeant yelled, his right hand raised.

The strollers regarded the horse soldiers with distaste and hurried out of the plaza. Foothills was in the state of Tennessee and had lost many fathers and sons to Union bullets. The sight of blue uniforms in the plaza was not therefore welcome – except to the madam and her girls who were interested only in the colour of men's money.

Carey's eyes showed distaste as he regarded the women, then concern as he detected a murmur of low excitement from the men. He turned in the saddle to look at the troopers. They were surveying the smiling women with either embarrassment, amusement or outright lust. The madam beamed and the whores, at a discreet signal from her, rose from the chairs and adopted sensuous postures, leaning against the wall and doorway, hanging smiles of invitation on their harshly pretty faces.

'Welcome to Foothills, Lieutenant,' the madam greeted. 'And to your men. The hotel and everything in it is at your service.'

A red-haired trooper tilted his forage cap to a jaunty angle and whispered to the red-faced youngster beside him: 'Reckon we're the ones to do the serving, eh, Fred?'

The sergeant glared at him. 'Hold your tongue, trooper,' he rasped.

The soldier grimaced as Carey touched his cap vizor. 'Obliged, ma'am,' the lieutenant said. 'But we don't have the time to rest up. We're on the trail of four men we believe headed this way.

One of them farms locally. His name is Edward Binns.'

'Ed Binns used to be a regular at the hotel, lieutenant,' the madam replied as the girls continued to pose beguilingly for the benefit of the soldiers. 'Until he upped and stole one of my . . . entertainers. Married her, would you believe? They farm a place ten, maybe twelve miles out in the hills.'

She pointed a well-manicured finger down the street in the direction the troop was headed, towards the scarlet sun dipping over the peaks of the Great Smoky Mountains.

'Did Binns and three other men come through town today, ma'am?' Carey asked.

The madam shrugged, heaving her immense bosom. 'I wouldn't know, lieutenant. You're in Tennessee now. Lots of folks hereabouts didn't do much mourning on account of what happened to the President. We've been rushed off our feet all day.'

Two of the girls pulled faces at the lie, but quickly rearranged their features as the madam shot them a warning glance.

'Off their feet and on their backs,' the red-headed trooper muttered.

The sergeant treated him to another piercing look and the soldier avoided meeting the non-com's rebuking eyes.

'Well, I guess we'd best push on to the Binns farm, sergeant,' Carey said.

The sergeant sighed silently and nodded. 'I think that's wise, sir,' he said with a side-long glance at the preening whores.

'Move them out,' Carey instructed.

The sergeant gave a hand signal, then yelled: 'Troooooop, fooorwaaard!'

The officer urged his mount along the street, choosing to ignore an angry-looking man of middle years who lounged in the saloon doorway and spat pointedly into the street. The column of troopers moved off into the dust raised by the leading horse. With the exception of the red-headed man, who placed a finger to his lips as the soldiers behind him were forced to swerve around his horse.

'*You're nuts!*' one of the two back-markers mouthed at the man.

His only response was to grin broadly towards the women in front of the hotel. They had dropped their phony attitudes of allure as they watched the departure of the soldiers. But when the madam called their attention to the man who had stayed behind, their bodies and faces began to emanate voluptuous promise once more. But no words were spoken until the horse soldiers were hidden in the cloud of their own dust, cantering clear of the town limits. Then, grinning, the red-headed man slid from his horse, leaving the animal to its own devices as he climbed up on to the sidewalk. He halted in front of the madam and doffed his cap.

'Right ill-mannered of the lieutenant to refuse the hospitality of your house, ma'am.' he said. 'I was brung up different to him.'

Up close, he could see that the madam's smile did not extend to her eyes. They surveyed him with glinting avariciousness.

'When were you last paid, soldier?' she wanted to know.

'Less than a week ago, ma'am,' he replied, having to make an effort to keep looking at the madam as the girls watched him with eager eyes. 'And I still got last month's pay. Been saving up for a day like this.'

'Which one do you like?' the madam invited.

Released so that his eyes could wander at will over the smiling faces and thrusting bodies of the girls, the soldier shrugged. 'I ain't one to show favouritism, ma'am,' he said. 'Money ain't all I been saving up.'

The madam nodded knowingly. 'Seems like the army's learning something from the navy,' she said, ushering the soldier into the murky shade of the hotel lobby.

The girls moved hurriedly in his wake. The madam stood on the sidewalk for a moment more, staring with a steely gaze into the settling dust behind the soldiers. Then she worked a great deal of saliva into her mouth and spat it forcefully into the horse tracks of the street.

The man in the saloon doorway laughed. 'And I thought you was a lady!' he called.

She glared hatefully across the plaza at him. 'Why don't you come on over and prove you're a man?' she invited.

The man hoisted his glass of foaming beer. 'I got six kids to prove it,' he said. 'I don't want no clap. Just cheers.'

He drank thirstily as the madam whirled and stormed into the hotel lobby.

CHAPTER EIGHT

LIEUTENANT Carey used only a hand signal to halt the troop at the crest of a rise, then raked his eyes over the small farmstead nestling in a shallow valley ahead. It was full night now, but the moon was at the threequarters and shed more than enough silvery blue light to illuminate the scene. There was a small, single storey house with a buckboard parked in the yard out front. To one side was a long barn with an empty corral behind it. All around were fields, most tilled for wheat, two given over to pasture. A single lighted window showed at the front of the house; the only sign of occupation. For in every other respect, the spread had a rundown, deserted look. And this impression was heightened by the solid silence which lay heavily across the valley. Against this stillness, every slight sound made by the soldiers or their horses seemed amplified out of all proportion.

'That must be the place,' Carey whispered.

The sergeant finished his survey of the unmoving scene below. 'Reckon you're right, sir. We come at least ten miles from town.'

'I think we'll dismount, fan out and go in carefully,' Carey said reflectively.

The sergeant was not impressed by the plan. 'If you think that's best, sir.'

Carey looked at the sergeant harshly, showing his distaste for a man who would question his orders. 'It's what I think, sergeant,' he hissed. 'This isn't a battlefield. There's a woman in there. Maybe some children. Apart from which, it's necessary to take these men alive.'

'Whatever the lieutenant says,' the sergeant acknowledged, his tone suggesting he was still against the plan, but was prepared to go along with it because of the younger man's higher rank. He turned in the saddle and beckoned the troopers into a tight group so he would not have to raise his voice. 'All right, we spread out in a line along the front of the house,' he instructed. 'We go in on foot, leading the horses. Nobody gets trigger happy unless the lieutenant or I give the word.'

His eyes suddenly narrowed and he did a double-take at the faces of the troopers. 'Where the hell is Clancy?' he hissed.

The young trooper who had ridden beside the deserter was suddenly aware that all eyes were turned towards him. He cleared his throat nervously. 'He got an ache, sergeant,' he said. 'He held back to relieve it. Says he'll catch us up.'

The sergeant's colouration turned from red to purple. 'I'll have the bastard court-martialled, 'he rasped. 'No, first I'll skin him alive and have what's left of him court-martialled.'

'Save it, sergeant!' Carey ordered. 'We have more pressing business to attend to. Form up and let's move.'

Leather slapped and harness jingled as the troopers slid from their saddles and spread out in a line across the ridge of the hill. Carey waited with mounting impatience and nervousness for the formation to be completed, then drew the Henry rifle from the saddle boot and started down the slope On either side of him the men set off, in a straggled line of advance.

They had reached the side of the yard when the door of the house was flung open and a woman's voice sounded.

'Far enough, soldier boys!' she called harshly. 'No man gets any closer to me unless I tell him he can.'

The troopers saw her as a silhouette against the yellow lamp light. The shotgun she held against her shoulder in a steady aim was just as clearly defined against the bright background. The men looked towards Carey and pulled up short as he halted.

Mona Binns was a handsome woman of almost thirty. She had long red hair and green eyes which were filled with grim determination as she surveyed the line of uniformed figures. Her dress was crudely made and tight-fitting, emphasising her ample curves as she stepped out into the yard.

'Good evening,' Carey greeted, struggling to keep nervousness out of his tone. 'You're Mrs Binns?'

The woman had been raking the gun back and forth along the line of men. Now she drew a bead on the lieutenant.

'If that's all you want, I'm Mona Binns,' she replied. 'You get that for free. Now get off my property.'

A wan-faced corporal thought he heard a faint scratching sound and shot a glance towards the barn at the side of the yard. It was rotting away. The roof was lop-sided and there were many holes in the side where lengths of timber had fallen or been torn off. Even from a distance of several yards it was possible to smell the musky odour of decay. It was not possible to see the four pairs of eyes peering through the holes.

'It's not quite as easy as that, Mrs Binns,' Carey said, his voice a little hoarse from trying to keep it pitched at an even tone. 'We've come for your husband and his three companions.'

Four gun muzzles were rested on the time-softened wood surrounding the holes.

'I haven't seen Ed in weeks,' Mona shouted.

Carey looked at the sergeant, who shrugged, indicating that the officer had called the initial action and would have to follow through on his own.

'You've only got to look at the place,' Mona went on. 'Easy to see Ed's got more important things to do than take care of the farm. Go look for him somewhere else, soldier boy. And when you find him, tell him to call in at the cat house on his way back. He'll need a replacement.'

In the fetid darkness of the barn, Carstairs grinned behind his pointing rifle. 'She almost sounds as if she means that, old boy,' he whispered.

Binns, only a few feet from Carstairs' position, did not allow himself to be distracted from his aim as he drew a bead on the red faced sergeant. 'If she gets rid of those troopers, she can say whatever the hell she wants,' he replied with soft-voiced conviction.

'Looks like it's gonna take more than words to send 'em on their way,' Monahan muttered.

Logan sweated and tugged at the crutch piece of his tight pants.

'Government business, Mrs Binns,' Carey said. 'It's necessary we search the house.'

He injected authority into his voice. Mona matched his tone.

'What's in it is my business, mister.'

Carey swallowed hard and took a step forward. Many of the troopers followed his example, palms sweating as they gripped reins and rifles.

'I warned you!' Mona screamed and squeezed one trigger of the shotgun.

Buckshot exploded from one of the two barrels and dirt showered up a foot in front of Carey. A yell of anger erupted from her mouth as the recoil of the gun thudded her back against the doorframe. Horses reared and the troopers struggled to hold them.

'Come on!' Carey shouted, letting go of his own mount and racing full-tilt towards the doorway.

The troopers followed his example, lumbering across the yard, rifles positioned to pour lead into the house but not daring to fire until the order was given.

'Saddle the nags, Ed,' Carstairs instructed.

'The hell with that,' Binns retorted angrily, leaning forward and firing through the hole. 'It's *my* wife those guys are goin' after.'

A trooper pitched forward, blood gushing from the side of his head, and the charge faltered as men whirled to face an attack from the flank.

'I told you!' Monahan yelled. 'I goddamn told you. We shoulda beat it in the first place!'

He fired out into the yard and another trooper was hit, spinning away beneath the trampling hooves of a panicked horse. A hail of bullets thudded into the timber of the barn as Logan fired a wild shot.

'Horses, Jack!' Carstairs ordered.

'Aw, I can shoot good as the rest,' Logan complained, pumping another shot through his hole.

'You hit the lousy buckboard again, stupid!' Monahan barked. 'Get the lousy horses.'

More bullets thudded into the side of the barn, some penetrating the areas where the timber was completely rotten. Logan scuttled quickly to the stalls at the far end of the barn, where four horses snorted and stamped in fright as shots exploded in the dark air, pungent with the fumes of burnt powder.

As he struggled to calm the frightened animals, Carstairs, Binns and Monahan alternately fired through the holes and ducked down low. Three uniformed figures were sprawled in the dust of the yard, one of them wailing his agony as he clutched at the spongy red pulp where his nose had been. Loose horses charged into each other as they raced to get away from the noise and smell of death. The side of the barn was pocked with yellow scars where bullets had splintered the wood and more appeared by the moment as the troopers poured lead towards the decaying building. Answering fire was exploded towards them, but they were no longer easy targets. They crouched in cover, behind the corner of the house, fences, a water barrel and the buckboard.

'What about those horses?' Carstairs demanded as he pumped out a shot, silencing the screams of the wounded man. His bullet entered the trooper's open mouth and burrowed deep into his brain.

'Bastards won't stand still,' Logan whined.

'Maybe we should ask the soldier boys to hold off 'til you quieten them?' Monahan suggested wryly, firing a shot which punctured the water barrel.

'Some of 'em made the house!' Binns yelled hysterically.

'But not Mona, Ed,' Monahan pointed out. 'They got other things on their minds.'

He and Carstairs fired simultaneously, and a uniformed form rolled into view from behind the barrel. Blood from two gaping wounds in his forehead poured out to tint the pool of spilled water.

Carey leaned out from the lighted doorway and fired three times in quick succession, seeing wood splinters fly. Then the Henry's pump action jammed and he drew back with a curse.

A trooper behind the buckboard emptied his rifle and fumbled to reload as an answering volley of shots thudded into the tail-gate. He whirled around, naked fear on his face, as he heard running footfalls. He brought the rifle up and almost squeezed the trigger at the ample frame of the sergeant as the non-com dropped down beside him.

'Christ, I thought you was one of them!' he said fearfully.

'That why you keep following me to the latrines?' the sergeant asked wryly, peering towards the barn.

'Sergeant, why don't we – '

Three shots had sounded together. The trooper looked at the sergeant in surprise, then toppled forward. Blood bubbled up through an enormous hole in the back of his head. The sergeant looked ruefully at the smaller hole in the side of the buckboard.

'Nothing but matchwood,' he said softly. 'Don't make nothing like they used to.'

Carey worked the action of the Henry loose and started to lean out to aim at the barn. But he froze as the muzzle of the shotgun was pressed against the nape of his neck.

'You stop it, or I kill you,' Mona ordered, not shouting, but her words and the menace of the tone were clearly discernible against the background of gunfire.

'You tried once before, ma'am,' Carey said throatily, cursing himself for ignoring the danger of the woman.

'A person's luck can change,' she replied. 'Tell them to stop.'

She applied pressure to the gun and Carey had to brace himself against the door frame to keep from being pushed out into the open.

'You must love him a whole lot,' Carey said tightly, stalling for time to think.

'I hate his guts,' Mona answered venomously. 'But if I don't help him, he'll kill me.'

'He won't get the chance,' Carey promised hopefully.

Mona eased up on the pressure, then rammed the gun muzzle hard into Carey's flesh. 'I'm not taking that chance, mister,' she hissed. 'Tell them to stop!'

Carey had used up all the time he was going to be allowed. And he had decided he was not brave enough to become a dead hero. 'Sergeant!'

The sergeant pumped off a final shot. 'Sir?'

'Cease fire.'

The non-com started to turn. 'Cease what?'

'Do it!' Carey ordered, fear feeding strength to his anger.

The sergeant completed his turn and saw the helplessness of Carey's position. 'Cease fire!' he yelled. 'Cease fire!'

The shooting continued for a few moments, then faltered and finally trailed away to distant echoes. There were a few seconds of eerie silence, made more intense by the sudden stillness from the barn.

'What now, ma'am?' Carey asked.

He wanted to turn around, but didn't trust the woman's state of nerves. Any unasked for gesture might panic her into squeezing the trigger of the pressing shotgun. Had he been able to see her confused expression, he would have realised she had thought no further ahead than this point. But abruptly, she reached a decision.

'Ed!' she shouted.

In the barn, Logan was saddling the fourth horse. He had been so intent on the chore that he failed to realise the gunfire had stopped. The sudden shout against the silence startled him.

'That's Mona!' Binns rasped in surprise, peering out across the slumped forms of the dead troopers, trying to detect a movement in the lighted doorway of the house.

'Sure sounds like a woman,' Monahan muttered wryly, feeding fresh shells into his rifle.

'Unless we shot the balls off a trooper,' Carstairs suggested.

'Finished,' Logan whispered, tightening the final cinch, then tugging at his pants.

'Mona?' Binns roared at the top of his voice.

'Saddle up and move out!' his wife called.

'What's happened, Mrs Binns?' Carstairs demanded in his well-modulated voice.

'I got the officer at the end of a gun. Move out before he gets brave.'

Carey was considering such an action. He could see several of his men, crouched in cover and although their eyes were merely faint pin-pricks of reflected light, he sensed the scorn arrowing towards him. But the pressure of the double-muzzled shotgun was a harsh warning against an impulsive move.

'What about you, Mona?' Binns shouted.

'Save the hearts and flowers, Ed!' Mona replied angrily.

There was a pause and every man with a view of the dilapidated barn looked at it apprehensively. When a horse snorted, many of the troopers snapped up their rifles to the aim.

'We're going,' Carstairs revealed calmly.

The troopers sighed as one man, but any sound they made was masked by the slap of leather and jingle of harness as the men mounted.

'No shooting, mister,' Mona said softly to Carey.

The lieutenant had to clear his throat before he could shout: 'Hold your fire, men!'

The doors were at one end of the barn. The sound of them crashing open was like a violent explosion: the beat of hooves against hard packed earth like a thousand echoes. Carstairs led the other three into the open at a gallop. Each man held a handgun and raked the yard with wild fire. The troopers flattened themselves to the ground or pressed their bodies against the walls of the house. Dirt spouted and wood splintered, but no further blood was spilled.

The riders fled around the rear of the house and started up the western side of the shallow valley. As the gunfire died away, the hoofbeats thundered like a rockfall. But soon, this sound had diminished into the distance.

'We gonna let 'em reach the Rockies before we go after them?' the sergeant asked sourly. He spat forcefully.

The shotgun continued to be pressed hard against the nape of Carey's neck. The sweat of fear and frustration stood out in bright beads on his forehead. He thought he hated the sergeant worse than the woman behind him.

'Don't get impatient, sergeant,' he called hoarsely. 'Let's all keep our heads.'

CHAPTER NINE

THE bodies of the four dead troopers lay side-by-side in the back of the buckboard, each wrapped in his bed blanket. A pale-faced young trooper with dried blood encrusting his right tunic sleeve sat on one side of the box seat, the reins held loosely in his left hand. Mona Binns sat beside him, her work-worn but still handsome face impassive as she regarded the column of mounted soldiers. She was not bound in any way.

Lieutenant Carey, the strain of suppressing his anger showing in the tightness of his mouth line and his upright posture in the saddle, sidled his horse close to the wagon. He pointedly refused to look at the woman.

'You understand what you're to do, Blake?' he snapped.

The young trooper attempted to raise his injured arm in a salute, but winced in pain and gave up. He nodded. 'I'm to arrange burial of the dead and treatment for myself, sir. I am then to put Trooper Clancy under arrest and escort him to Washington to await court martial proceedings.'

Carey nodded curtly. 'Mrs Binns is also under arrest. She has shown herself to be as guilty as her husband of complicity in the conspiracy.'

Mona tried to meet his eyes, but Carey had already started to turn away, heading for the leading position in the column of men. 'I don't know what you're talking about,' she said.

Carey completely ignored her as he took up his position and nodded to the sergeant.

'Let's move out,' the non-com instructed and the troopers heeled their mounts forward, following Carey around to the rear of the house, picking up the tracks left by the fleeing wanted men.

Blake clucked to the horse in the shafts and slapped the reins across the animal's back. The buckboard turned in a half circle and headed out of the yard and on to the trail which led to town. From time to time he cast furtive glances at the woman seated beside him, but she sat like a wax statue, not returning his interest nor showing any inclination to break the silence between them.

But he was glad she was there. She was not old enough, but in some respects she reminded the young trooper of his mother, whom he loved very dearly. So her presence was comforting in his pain and the unnerving knowledge that he was transporting four dead men through a dark night.

On Mona's part, the soldier at her side did not exist. As the buckboard started out on the trip to town, she had fleetingly considered making a try to rob him of his gun and shoot him. But she dismissed the thought, knowing she was incapable of such a cold-blooded act. Just as she had known, after the initial impulsive action of jamming the shotgun against the lieutenant's head, that she could not have pulled the trigger.

So, in this self-knowledge, she resigned herself to whatever the future held. It was her way, and always had been, to act impulsively and then await the consequences. It was how she had become a whore and then allowed Edward Binns to marry her. Neither had been worse than she expected, because she expected nothing. Her philosophy was that people were put on earth to be used, or to use other people. She placed herself in the former category.

Thus, when Ed and the others heard the approach of the horse soldiers, she had agreed without reluctance to play the part allotted to her in the plan. Only when she saw the bodies of the troopers slump to the ground, spouting blood, did her life-long revulsion for violence trigger the impulsive action which ended the slaughter. Now she withdrew into her shell again, awaiting the actions of others to sweep her along in the next phase of her life.

'Ma'am?' Blake said softly when they had put two miles or so between themselves and the farm.

She turned towards him, and he quickly looked ahead at the moonlit trail. 'Yes?'

'I don't hold it against you – what you did back there. He's your husband and you ought to help him out of a jam.'

Mona felt a stab of pity for the boy's ignorance and it showed in her green eyes. But he was too embarrassed to look at her and didn't see it. She did not enlighten him verbally.

Blake cleared his throat. 'Fact is, I wouldn't feel right locking you up, ma'am,' he said. 'Now when we get to Washington, I'm going to have to hand you over to the law. Guess we won't be staying long in Foothills, but I can imagine what the goalhouse is like. Lady didn't oughta spend even a minute in it, I'd say. Any place more comfortable you can stay if I put you on your honour not to run away?'

The offer did not lighten Mona's mood. She thought of Ed's brother Harry and the comfortable rooms above the drapery store. She thought especially of the snug bedroom where she had spent so many happy hours, both passion-filled and gentle. It would be nice to be with Harry again for awhile. Her love affair with him had started on an impulse and had provided the only moments of happiness she could remember in a long time. But what would it be like, being with Harry and knowing she was in danger of never seeing him again?

'What do you say?' the pale faced young trooper urged.

Mona reached her second decision in one night, and nodded emphatically as Blake glanced at her. 'I've got a place I can go,' she said.

'And you won't try to run away?'

'No, I promise,' she said, and meant it.

It was a paradox that Harry Binns was the sole reason why she would make no attempt to escape. For it was his solid respectability and determination to succeed in his Foothills drapery store which had first impressed Mona. Unlike the plan-a-day, anything-for-a-fast-buck methods of Ed, Harry was a stick-in-the-mud plodder. He had taken over the family business and was quite happy within its limited horizons. And even his love for his brother's wife did not alter the main course of the life he had plotted out for himself. If he had allowed it to do so, they would have run away together long ago. So what was the use of escaping when the only person in the world who meant anything to Mona was as firmly fixed in Foothills as the church and town bank?

'I'll trust you,' Blake said after a few moments of silent thought.

Mona nodded vacantly, her unintelligent mind concerned with Harry's possible reactions to the news she would bring him. And this worried her so much that when Blake halted the buckboard in the plaza of the silent and darkened town, she could not bring herself to knock on the front door of the store. She went to the rear, hopeful of finding the door there unlocked. It was not. So again she put herself in the hands of fate, and crouched down in the shelter of some empty cardboard cartons stacked against the wall. She silently rehearsed at least twenty ways to give Harry the news before sleep overtook her.

At a first floor window of the hotel, Adam Steele watched the buckboard come down the street and halt in the plaza. He saw the woman climb down and walk slowly towards the store bearing the name of one of the men he intended to kill. He didn't move, maintaining his vigil as the soldier angled the buckboard towards the funeral parlour, appropriately sited next door to the church. He saw the soldier knock on the window and watched as the timid-looking undertaker in a nightshirt emerged from a side door. The two men exchanged a few words, then transferred the blanket-wrapped bodies from the wagon to the parlour. It didn't take long. The men talked again, then the soldier left the wagon and horse in the care of the undertaker and approached the hotel, his gait revealing over-active nerves.

Steele fingered the ornate head of the tiepin decorating his neckerchief, sighed and moved away from the window to stretch out, fully clothed, on the narrow bed. The pin was the only bright and new looking thing about him now. His clothing was creased and grimed with trail dust and his face was heavily stubbled and streaked with sweat-crusted dirt. He could smell himself, and under any other circumstance, this would have disgusted him. But nothing was as important as killing the men who had lynched his father. Everything else paled into insignificance beside this.

'Clancy, I know you're in there!'

Steele was staring up at the ceiling with blank eyes as Blake's voice sounded out in the hallway. The words were accompanied by the heavy rap of knuckles on the door panel of the next room. A girl gave a low scream and a man groaned out of sleep.

'Who the hell's that?'

'Blake. The lieutenant sent me to arrest you for desertion. You coming quiet?'

'Aw, come back in the morning, feller,' the man in the next room moaned. 'We'll talk about it then.'

Blake banged his first on the door again. 'Open up before I break down the door.'

A door was flung open. 'You damage my property and I'll cut off your pecker and hang it outside for a sign.'

It was the madam, her voice quivering with anger.

'I got my duty to perform, ma'am,' Blake shot back at her, and banged on the door again. 'Clancy, come on out!'

Steele sighed and swung his legs over the edge of the bed. He went to the door and jerked it open. Outside, the hallway was dimly lit by a single lamp with the wick turned down low. Blake and the madam looked towards Steele and were both startled by his sudden appearance. Steele eyed the young trooper levelly, recalling how, not long ago, he would have found it necessary to kill him because of the colour of his uniform.

'I paid for a room in which I could sleep, trooper,' he said softly. 'I'd like to get my moneysworth.'

'I got my orders,' Blake shot back.

Steele nodded. 'Do you have to carry them out tonight?'

'The lieutenant said – '

'The lieutenant here?' Steele cut in.

'No.'

'So you're not impressing him,' Steele pointed out. 'Just annoying me.'

'And others,' the madam supplemented. Her body was hidden in the doorway of her room. Her face, spread with white cream, looked disembodied and ghost-like in the low lighting.

'I can't allow him to escape,' Blake said emphatically, hand resting on his holstered revolver.

'Clancy?' Steele called.

'Who the hell are you?' the man in the next room demanded.

'Nobody you'd know. Do you intend to go anywhere tonight?'

Clancy gave an obscene laugh. 'Everything I need is right here.'

The whore with him laughed. Steele looked questioningly at Blake.

'Why should I believe him?' the young trooper asked.

'You don't have to,' Steele replied. 'Just stay where you are and you've got him trapped.'

The trooper was not convinced. Then the door of the next room opened and Clancy, completely naked, looked out at Blake. 'Come on in, for Christsake,' the older trooper invited. 'Let's talk about it.'

'Quietly,' Steele suggested.

Clancy poked his head out through the doorway. He met Steele's blank-eyed stare, held it a moment, then shrugged. 'Like mice we'll be,' he said.

'He touches the girl, he'll have to pay,' the madam warned

from the far end of the hallway.

'Sure,' Clancy said. 'You coming, Johnnie?'

Blake's eyes widened and Clancy glanced over his shoulder and grinned. The girl he had bought for the night was standing on the bed, legs splayed and hands cupping her large breasts. She was completely naked, and smiling invitingly with her generous mouth. The glint in her eyes could have been lust or avariciousness as she surveyed another paying customer.

'Not yet, but breathing hard I guess,' Clancy said with a leer as he stood aside to allow Blake to enter the room.

The door closed.

'Don't you want any company, mister?' the madam called.

Steele nodded. 'The girl who's been here the longest. I already paid at the desk for her.'

'She hasn't been to see you yet?' the madam asked, puzzled.

'She'll be here at seven in the morning,' Steele replied, retreating into the room and closing the door.

'You like to get up early,' the madam called, and laughed before withdrawing into her own room.

Steele crossed to the window and looked out over the plaza towards the façade of the drapery store. It was still as dark as the other buildings of the town. He wondered momentarily about the woman who had come in on the buckboard with the trooper. And about the four bodies and the blood on Blake's limp right arm.

Then he stretched out on the bed and stared at the ceiling for a few seconds. He made his mind go as blank as his eyes, then closed his eyes. Sleep came easily to his weary body.

CHAPTER TEN

HARRY Binns was fat, forty and a practising Christian. He had a tidy mind and liked his life to run on well-ordered lines. Thus, when he opened the rear door of his premises to take out the ashes of yesterday's cooking fire, the shock at seeing Mona stretched out among the cartons was a very strong one indeed. For not only was it a traumatic departure from his daily routine, which was upsetting enough in itself. But the sight of the woman was an explicit reminder of the only two events in his life of which he was ashamed – being the brother of the no-good Edward and allowing himself to make free with the willing body of Edward's wife.

After glancing hurriedly at the windows overlooking the store's yard, he roused the sleeping woman and implored her to stay silent until he had ushered her into the stockroom.

Nobody saw what happened, because the only person watching the store was doing so from a window with no view of the rear. Adam Steele, his stubble thicker and his clothes even more crumpled after a night's sleep, kept a careful surveillance on the store's frontage, waiting for a sign that it was open for business. He was seated on the room's only chair, the presentation Colt Hartford resting across his knees. Behind him, the room was spartanly furnished – a bed, a bureau and a wardrobe in rough painted walls on one of which hung a crucifix.

There was a gentle, tentative knock on the door. He did not turn around, but craned forward and glanced towards the east. He judged the sun to be in its seven o'clock position.

'Come in,' he called.

A girl of about twenty entered and halted in the doorway. She was slim and pretty, with shoulder length black hair and brown eyes filled with fear as she regarded the back of the man seated at the window. Her white dress was cut on simple lines, close-fitting enough to show she wore little or nothing beneath it.

'You wanted me, Mr. Steele,' she said nervously. 'My name's Jennie.'

Steele glanced quickly over his shoulder, his eyes showing nothing of what he felt upon seeing the girl. 'If you're the one who's been here the longest, I do.'

Jennie closed the door. 'Is a year long enough for you?' she asked.

'I reckon,' Steele replied, concentrating upon the store across the plaza.

The girl's dress was buttoned from its high neck to its low hem. She inserted the index finger of her left hand beside the top button and ran her hand down. The buttons popped open in rapid succession, all the way to the bottom. When she straightened up, the dress gaped wide. She wore nothing beneath it. Her brown crested breasts were small and retained their conical shape. Her stomach had a youthful flatness and her slim legs quivered slightly with a muscular spasm. The redness of her bodily hair gave the lie to her long tresses. Her firm white flesh showed several old bruises left by an over-enthusiastic patron of the house.

'You want anything special, Mr. Steele?' she asked softly, arranging her features in an expression of professional allure.

Steele meant to glance quickly over his shoulder, but the girl's nakedness captured and held his attention. 'Hey,' he said hoarsely. 'The bathroom's down the hall.'

Jennie showed her confusion. 'But madam said – '

'That lady thinks all men want the same thing,' Steele cut in with a sigh, and dragged his gaze away, resuming his study of Binns' Drapery.

'Well, don't they?' Jennie asked, continuing to hold her dress wide. 'You paid.'

'For talk,' Steele said.

'I've been paid for some funny things, but – '

'So broaden your mind,' Steele interrupted, unprovoked by the hint of annoyance which had entered her tone.

'I do most things better with no clothes on,' Jennie said, softening her voice. 'Even talk.'

'But I won't listen so well,' Steele muttered. 'Cover yourself.'

The girl was offended. Steele had hurt her professional pride He didn't even want to look at her body. But she didn't make the mistake of rebuking him. As she rebuttoned the dress, she consoled herself with the thought that the man, no matter how tough he looked, had to be a fag.

'What do you want to know?' she asked when the fastening was complete.

Steele was fingering the head of the tiepin. He saw movement behind the glass door of the store across the plaza and leaned forward suddenly. The man who shot the bolts at the top and bottom of the door appeared only as a blurred shadow from such a distance.

'Man at the drapery,' Steele asked, leaning back in the chair. 'He the Binns with his name over the door?'

Jennie grimaced. 'He's too mean to employ help. If you figure to buy anything, watch him. He gives short change.'

'He was out of town recently, wasn't he?'

As fully dressed as she ever was when in the hotel, Jennie leaned her back against the door in the age old pose of the oldest profession. 'What if he was?'

'I figure he went to Washington,' Steele said.

The girl realised she was wasting her time in trying to interest a man who didn't even want to look at her. She moved wearily away from the door and draped herself across the bed. There was nothing seductive in the action. She merely seemed tired. 'You sound as if you know it all, already.'

Steele whirled around on the chair. For a moment, she hiked up the hem of her dress and filled her lungs with air, thrusting forward her small breasts. But the bright anger in Steele's dark eyes swamped her sensuality. She hauled herself into a stiff sitting posture and dropped her nervous gaze to the bare boards of the floor.

Steele kept his voice low. 'Be grateful if you'd just answer the questions, lady,' he said.

Jennie shrugged her slim shoulders. 'Okay. If Binns went anyplace, he went to Washington. He goes to Washington a lot. On buying trips. All the dresses he stocks have Washington labels on them.'

The man's anger died and he smiled at the girl. But only with his mouth. The expression had no warmth in it, for the dark eyes had become menacingly blank. This mood frightened Jennie more than his fury. Anxious to please him, she swung her feet to the floor and stood up, raising a hand to the top button of her dress.

'Sure,' she said. 'This one has got one in it. You want to see, Mr Steele?'

He shook his head. 'No thanks,' he replied wryly. 'I already saw what was in the dress. It didn't do anything for me.'

She whirled and stormed to the door. She jerked it open and, with her escape route secured, allowed herself the luxury of venting her anger.

'Mister, there ain't nothing will do anything for a man like you,' she hurled at him.

The door was slammed and Jennie's bare footfalls in the hallway were heavy, a further sign of her rage. The taunt left Steele unmoved as he turned to look out of the window again.

'There's something, lady,' he said softly to himself. 'There's something for sure.'

Over at the store, Harry Binns listened with mounting agitation to Mona's account of what had happened out at his brother's farmstead.

'You did that?' he asked, aghast.

It was a large, well-stocked store, with a neat, businesslike look about it. There was a counter down one side, backed by shelves and glass-fronted drawers filled with clothes, yarns, tapes and braids. Racks of dresses and suits, with a number of model dummies took up a great deal of space in front of the counter. Along the opposite wall and at the rear was more shelving, stacked with bolts of cloth. It was neat, clean and colourful and Mona, in her ill-cut and dirt-streaked dress, looked out of place in the store.

Binns was well aware of this fact and, since he was now opened for business, was anxious to be rid of the woman. But at least he had been able to place himself on one side of the counter and Mona on the other, and this was an important achievement. For, as far as the citizens of Foothills were aware, Harry's low regard for his brother had sunk still further when he married a whore. And, as Harry had been at pains to state on many occasions, he only allowed Mona in his store because of family ties.

'I had to, darling,' Mona answered, not seeing Harry's slight wince at the endearment. 'There were four dead as it was. If it had gone on, how many would have been killed?'

Her eyes implored understanding from Harry. He could not hold her gaze, and saw only the dirt beneath her broken fingernails as she brushed a strand of matted hair from in front of her eye.

'Ed might have been among them,' he put in suddenly, aware he had to say something.

Mona reached impulsively across the counter and clasped one of his pudgy hands. He glanced nervously down towards the display windows, grateful that no one was passing on the plaza. Sweat broke out on his forehead and he jerked his hand from beneath hers.

'Please, Mona. Not here.'

Mona nodded, understanding his embarrassment while not suspecting its depths. 'He's as good as dead to us, Harry. Even if he gets away from the soldiers, he'll never dare to come back to the farm.'

She looked hard into his soft, moist, fleshy, unhandsome face, love shining in her green eyes.

'And what about the soldier who brought you into town?' Harry asked, swallowing hard as a wagon lumbered across the plaza.

'I thought if I offered him money,' Mona blurted out suddenly. 'You have some money, don't you, Harry? He might let me go. Tell his officers I escaped.'

The wife of the undertaker halted on the sidewalk outside and peered through the thick lenses of her eyeglasses at the window display. Binns was sure the woman intended to enter the store and he was panicked into hasty thought.

'Go back to the farm, Mona,' he said quickly, almost stammering as the words spilled over his trembling lower lip. 'I'll talk to the soldier. I'll come out tonight and tell you what he says.'

The undertaker's wife was dividing her attention between the contents of her purse and a red skirt draped in the window.

'That's wonderful, darling,' Mona exclaimed, reaching out for his hand again. But he drew it away. 'You will come?'

Binns nodded. 'Best if you go out the back way,' he implored.

'Yes. Yes, Harry. I'll wait for you. Please come as soon as you can.'

She backed away towards the door in the rear wall which gave on to the stockroom. Just before she went from sight, she raised a hand to her lips and blew him a kiss. Binns groaned and waved her away with an angry gesture before turning to look with trepidation towards the front of the store as the bell jangled at the top of the door.

The unresponsive eyes of Adam Steele locked on Binns' gaze and held it for several seconds. When the sweating storekeeper was finally able to look elsewhere, Steele crossing the threshhold and half turning to close the door, he saw that the undertaker's wife was moving away, eyeing her purse ruefully.

'Yes, sir?' Binns asked anxiously. 'Something I can do for you?'

Steele approached him casually, glancing disinterestedly to left and right at the colourful displays. 'Reckon so.'

The man looked tough, but that was nothing new. To the soft and portly Binns, most men looked tough. But there was something else about this one – a certain quiet menace that seemed to emanate from him without needing physical expression or an aggressive action to mark it.

'Happy to be of service,' Binns offered, blinking and shooting a glance towards the rear of the store as the back door of the building was closed with a slight sound. 'What precisely are you looking for?'

Steele halted immediately in front of Binns and rested the Colt Hartford along the counter, gripping it lightly in his gloved hands. Neither his expression nor his tone changed. 'The four bastards who lynched my father,' he said. 'Hear you were one of them.'

Binns gulped and staggered backwards, coming up hard against the display shelf behind him. A sign, which proclaimed CLOSED FOR LUNCH, fell to the floor. All colour drained from his cheeks and his lips were suddenly very red by contrast.

'What . . . what . . . do you me . . . mean?' he stammered.

Steele spun the rifle a half turn and jabbed it forward. The muzzle made a dent in the storekeeper's pot belly and held it. Binns stopped breathing.

'Your name Binns?' Steele asked.

The fat man's terrified gaze swept towards the front of the store, but the plaza was as empty as a summer sky. The blank-eyed stare of the stranger recaptured his trembling attention.

'Yes . . . ye . . . yes. But . . . I don't – '

'Buy your supplies in Washington?'

Binns nodded vigorously and ran a finger along his top lip. New beads of sweat were immediately squeezed out to replace those wiped away. 'What's this all . . . all about, mister?'

'Something you haven't got to worry about – for long.'

Steele suddenly withdrew the rifle. Binns experienced a moment of relief. Then the muzzle was driven towards him again, smashing hard into his middle. Air gushed out of his lungs in a gasp and he started to fold over double. Steele jerked the rifle clear. He raised it and brought it down hard. The barrel cracked against Binns' skull and crushed his forehead against the counter top. The fat man went limp and crumpled out of sight behind the counter.

Steele pursed his lips in a silent whistle and toyed with the lobe of his left ear as he glanced around the store. His blank eyes roved along the shelves of rolled cloth and settled on a reel of black serge. After a quick glance out over the deserted plaza, he rested the Colt Hartford against the counter and moved across to the shelves. The cloth was heavy – several yards long and a yard and a half wide wound around a wooden reel.

He swung it over the counter and vaulted after it. There was a lot of blood in Binns' mouth, where his teeth had sunk into his tongue. The space behind the counter was restricted, but the area was not visible from the street. Steele's expression showed nothing of what he thought as he unwound the entire length of material and began to bind it tightly around the fat man. He started at the feet and worked upwards. Binns snapped open his eyes and spat out blood. He stared in horror at Steele, then down at his body, bound from feet to neck in the material. He could not move a muscle.

'Please, I – '

Steele grabbed the man's thinning hair and jerked his head clear of the ground. Binns gave a low scream which became a muffled groan as a width of cloth was jerked across his bloodied mouth. A further series of groans came from the depths of his helplessness as Steele wound the material around his head twice more, then fastened it with a pin taken from a display box.

His work complete, he picked up the CLOSED FOR LUNCH sign and slid over the counter. He found a pencil stub near the cash drawer and began to alter the sign, ignoring the pathetic sounds from the man on the floor.

'My father died quick,' he said casually as Binns' sounds of distress grew weaker. 'But I reckon he suffered a lot before the table was finally kicked from under him. Just the thought of dying that way would have terrified a man like him.'

He finished working on the sign and leaned forward to peer over the counter. Binns summoned every iota of strength left in him and managed to roll over on to his side. He gave a gasp, desperately trying to empty his lungs of useless, oxygen-starved air. It finished as a death rattle and his dead body rolled back and was still.

Steele picked up the rifle and turned towards the front of the store as the signal bell jangled above the door.

'It's all right, I've seen the soldier and he says – '

Mona pulled up short and curtailed her excited announcement as she saw the figure of Steele approaching her. Steele smiled at her with his mouth, recognising her as the woman who had come to town on the buckboard last night.

'Oh, isn't Harry – Mr Binns – here?' she asked.

Steele touched his hat brim with a gloved hand. 'He had a little trouble with his breathing, ma'am,' he replied. 'He's lying down.'

Mona's excitement died and she regarded Steele with heavy suspicion. 'You aren't the doctor,' she accused.

Steele sidled around her and opened the door, hanging the sign on it. 'No, ma'am,' he confirmed. 'Binns and I had some business to do. It's all wrapped up now. Good day.'

He stepped out on to the sidewalk and closed the door on Mona's confusion. She could not read, from the inside, the sign which swung gently in the draught from the closing door. One word had been scored out, and another added.

It read: CLOSED FOR EVER.

CHAPTER ELEVEN

CLANCY and Blake sat on a sofa in a corner of the lobby as Steele entered from the street and crossed to the desk. The blood encrusted right sleeve of Blake's tunic hung limp and empty at his side. His arm was in a sling across his chest.

'Checking out, ma'am,' Steele told the over-painted madam behind the desk.

'Look, Blakey,' Clancy said earnestly. 'You made your mind up by telling the dame she could get lost. It's a lousy army, anyway. With the war over, what's the goddamn point? You're likely to get shipped out to some crummy patch of desert and get your hair lifted by a crazy drunk Indian.'

Steele had to pay for the greasy meal he had been served shortly after he arrived at the hotel the previous night.

'But the pay's regular,' Blake argued, wanting to be convinced.

Steele told the madam he would pass up breakfast.

Clancy snorted. 'It's so frigging small they can afford to give it to you regular. Why, I hear that in Texas a man can – '

Mona's scream carried clearly across the sunlit plaza. Steele calmly pocketed the loose change given him by the madam as she and the two troopers swung around to look out through the open doors. Mona's footfalls thudded against the hard-backed dirt of the plaza: then sounded hollowly against the planking of the sidewalk. She burst into the lobby and pulled up abruptly. Her face was drained of colour and her body trembled. The agony of her grief seemed to vibrate in the hot, still air. She raised her hand and pointed a quivering finger at Steele. Time stretched interminably as she summoned the strength to speak.

'He killed him!' she was finally able to rasp.

The trooper and the madam abruptly turned their shock-filled eyes towards Steele. His face was blank of expression as he backed over to a doorway at the foot of a flight of stairs. The rifle was held loose at his side, tilted slightly to point at the floor.

'He shouldn't have lynched my father, ma'am,' Steele said calmly.

Mona shook her head vigorously, continuing to point the finger of guilt at Steele. 'Harry's never harmed anybody in his life,' she flung at him.

Steele narrowed his eyes by a fraction, but in no other way did he show the traumatic effect the woman's statement had on him. She had called Binns *Harry*. The old timer had named one of the lynchers as *Ed* Binns. He kept his voice at an even pitch. 'I heard about him from an eye-witness, ma'am,' he said, his mind in a turmoil as he struggled to make himself believe that Harry was Ed called by another name in his home town. 'Binns was just one of them. I've got three more to settle with.'

Mona lowered her arm and brought herself under control. 'Where?' she demanded, knocking a strand of hair away from her right eye. 'Where is he supposed to have – '

'Washington,' Steele replied. 'Right after Lincoln was shot.'

Steele, the madam and the two troopers saw the confusion spread across Mona's handsome face, to be suddenly swamped by realisation. She gave a hysterical laugh which twisted her features into ugliness. 'You kill-crazy fool!' she shrieked. 'Harry was the wrong man. You murdered the wrong Binns. He hasn't been to Washington in weeks. It was Ed you wanted. My goddamn, no good husband Ed – Harry's brother.'

Steele was deserted by the capacity to hide his feelings behind an impassive mask. The awful knowledge that he had brought agonising death to an innocent man exploded on to his face in a colour-draining, immobilising expression of self-hatred. But as his eyes turned to each person in the lobby, imploring for understanding, begging for consolation, they found none.

Hoofbeats sounded out on the street. He looked through the doorway, beyond the voluptuous form of his accuser, and the sunlight seemed suddenly to darken. He fell back against the door and blinked. The harsh light of morning returned to full intensity and he saw the two riders starkly outlined against the buildings of the plaza. Both were travel-stained and weary looking. One of them was a mean-faced man in a frock coat. The other was Jim Bishop.

Steele snapped up the rifle and felt his emotions freeze as he turned his blank-eyed stare towards Mona.

'My father was innocent too,' he said, giving the door behind him a back-heel kick which crashed it open. 'It's a lousy world, ma'am.'

The two riders dismounted, flexing muscles stiffened by long hours in the saddle.

'Thanks for your custom,' the madam called as Steele backed out into the yard behind the hotel. 'Come again.'

Lovell and Bishop entered the lobby, brushing through between Mona and the doorframe. Both sensed the tension in the hot air, and looked from the open rear door to the madam.

'We're looking for a man,' the Washington detective announced.

Everyone looked at the newcomers and saw the evil of Lovell and the confusion of Bishop.

'You come to the wrong place, fellers,' the madam replied brightly. 'This is a cat house. I hear Aaron Ross over at the livery might accommodate you.'

Clancy grinned. Blake swallowed hard. Mona sagged against the doorpost. Lovell snapped the revolver from the holster at the front of his bent and levelled it as he approached the desk.

'Name's Adam Steele,' he snapped.

The madam had run a house for too long to be intimidated by a gun pointing at her ample bosom. 'Pleased to meet you,' she said, her eyes glittering as she held Lovell's resolute stare. 'Strange thing. We had a man with the same monicker staying here. He just checked out.'

Realisation hit Mona for a second, and the gasp she gave caused both Lovell and Bishop to swing towards her. 'Through there!' she shrieked, pointing a shaking finger. 'He went through there. Only seconds ago.'

When the two lawmen burst into the yard, both had revolvers in their fists, and the muzzles swung rapidly from side to side, covering the whole cluttered area. Eyes raked over boxes and trash baskets. Lovell waved his gun to one side and Bishop moved as directed, using his free hand and his feet to knock and kick over the rubbish. Lovell did the same on the other side of the yard.

They found nothing and looked angrily towards the stairway climbing up the rear of the hotel, and the two empty alleys leading off.

'I'll look up top,' Bishop said breathlessly, turning to the foot of the steps.

'Forget it!' Lovell snapped, heading into one of the alleys. 'He'd know he'd be trapped up there. Check that, then comb the whole frigging town.'

Bishop glanced up the stairway, then shrugged and went into the alley Lovell had indicated.

Steele remained motionless, stretched out full length in the hot sun on the roof, until the sound of the lawmen's angry footfalls had faded. Then he wriggled backwards, away from the roof's edge. He raised his head, but not his body, and glanced around. The otherwise flat surface of the roof was broken by two smoking chimneys and a number of trapdoor frames. He stayed as flat to the sun-heated boarding as he could, rotating his body until the nearest trapdoor was only inches from his face.

He could hear voices in the bedroom below.

'Now you won't forget?' a man said timorously. 'Anyone starts to poke fun at me, you tell 'em.'

A girl trilled with laughter. 'That I will, Mr Ross,' she said, and Steele's mouthline tightened as he recognised Jennie's voice. 'It's all been just rumours about you. Ain't no question but that a girl knows which way to turn with you.'

'That's fine,' the man replied. 'Yes, that's fine. Goodbye, Miss Jennie. See you again soon.'

Footfalls sounded. 'Hope so, Mr Ross,' Jennie said. 'I'll be ready and willing.' A door opened and closed. 'You smelly little creep,' she finished softly.

Steele waited a few more seconds, to make sure the girl did not have a customer immediately after Ross, then inserted his fingers under the edge of the trapdoor and inched it up. He pushed the rifle barrel through the crack, and sighted down it. The hinges creaked and Jennie stared up in frightened surprise.

The bed was immediately beneath the trapdoor and she was spread across it, on top of the counterpane. She was completely naked now, the dress draped over a chair close to the bed. Her body was spread-eagled, as if in readiness to be entered rather than in relaxation after the act. Perhaps because of her profession, which made modesty hypocritical, or because the sight of the pointing rifle terrified her, she remained frozen in position, every secret place of her naked flesh open to Steele's indifferent gaze.

'Some you lay for, some you lie to,' Steele said softly, opening the trapdoor wider and then keeping her covered as he hauled himself into a sitting position, legs hanging through the square hole.

'What's that supposed to mean?' she demanded.

'Drapery store man hasn't been to Washington in weeks,' he replied, gripping the Colt Hartford in one hand as he folded up the trapdoor.

She shrugged, the gesture rippling the flesh of her shoulders and quivering the mounds of her breasts. 'I get paid for pleasing men, mister,' she said. 'You paid and I told you what you wanted to know. I thought it made you happy.'

'It made me a murderer,' he told her.

She gasped as he suddenly dropped through the opening, drawing the door closed after him. His boots sank into the bed at the side of each naked hip and the rifle muzzle jabbed lightly at the white skin of her throat.

'Now I want something for free,' he warned softly.

She smiled and drew up her knees, splaying her thighs wider, her feet hooking around his ankles. 'Help yourself,' she invited, cupping her breasts, stacking the flesh so that the nipples pointed up at him.

'No,' he told her. 'Help from you.'

CHAPTER TWELVE

FOOTHILLS was not a large town, but the thoroughness with which Lovell and Bishop searched it kept them engaged with the gruelling chore until well past dusk. On each occasion when their paths crossed, Lovell's temper was darker and more explosive. Because of this, which indicated the Washington detective was likely to shoot Steele on sight, Bishop's concern deepened – for it was his intention to take the wanted man alive to stand trial.

It was after seven when the unsuccessful search ended and the two lawmen met in front of Aaron Ross's livery stable. Both were bleary-eyed, with haggard faces and bowed shoulders.

'That's about it,' Bishop said with a deep sigh that was part a sign of weariness, part of relief. 'There's no place else to look.'

Lovell eyed the deputy sheriff with disgust. 'It was a mistake letting you ride with me,' he snarled. 'If I'd been alone, he wouldn't have ducked out so quick. You, he knows.'

He spun around and strode into the livery stable. Bishop glanced up and down the street leading off the plaza and followed the city detective. The place smelled of kerosene, straw and horse droppings. In the light of two lamps, Clancy was adjusting the bridle of a saddled horse. Blake was being helped in readying his own mount by a short, thin man with a bald head and melancholy eyes. He was Ross, and his sad eyes became fixed on Lovell's glowering face as the lawmen halted in the doorway.

'His horse is still in the stall, marshal,' the little man announced with forced enthusiasm. 'He ain't been in since you first come.'

'I told you, I'm not a marshal,' Lovell hurled at Ross, then loped across the stable to the stall the liveryman had indicated with a nod.

Steele's bay gelding nuzzled the detective's hand eagerly, then snorted when he found no sugar. Ross gave the injured trooper a leg up into his saddle.

'You ready, Clancy?' Blake asked anxiously.

'Sure am,' the older trooper replied, grasping hold of his mount's bridle.

Bishop stepped out of the entrance to allow passage for the troopers. Then a flash of metal caught his eye and he took a step forward, knowing he would be too late. 'Lovell, don't!' he yelled.

The gelding started to rear, sensing danger. But Lovell was an expert with the knife, fast and deadly. He plunged it towards the animal's head, allowing for instinctive movement, and angling the blade at the right degree. The deadly point penetrated deep into the horse's staring right eye, the cant of the blade directing it incisively into the brain. There was a thin, high wail, then a massive gout of blood which arched across Lovell's ducked shoulder. The detective retained his grip on the knife handle and the blade came free with a sucking sound as the dead animal collapsed to the floor of the stall.

Clancy and Blake spoke softly to the trembling horses, calming their agitation at the smell of blood. Then they joined Ross and Bishop in treating Lovell to stares of revulsion. The detective turned slowly, and swung his mean-eyes glare from Clancy to Blake and back again.

'Law's business, soldiers,' he said, wiping the bloody blade on the bedroll hanging next to Steele's saddle. 'Army ought to mind its own.'

'Sure, mister, sure,' Blake blurted.

'Don't pay no heed to the uniforms,' Clancy said. 'We ain't in the army no more.'

Blake led the way out of the stable, and Clancy was hard on his heels. The beat of galloping hooves was the only sound against the quiet of the town. Soon, even this was swallowed up by distance.

'My God,' Ross gasped, trembling. 'What will I tell him if he comes back?'

'That his horse was lucky,' Lovell replied softly, sliding the knife back into its sheath at his armpit. 'For him, it won't be fast.'

He moved to the door and Ross stumbled hurriedly out of his

path. He leaned against the doorframe and started to roll a cigarette, looking with meanly angry eyes at a glass-sided hearse which emerged from the side of the undertaker's parlour. It was hauled by a high-stepping pair and driven by somebody in a hooded cloak. Lovell lit the cigarette and stepped up on to the sidewalk. Bishop followed him, knuckling tired eyes. As the hearse rolled by and turned onto the street heading west out of town, both men could see in through the glass side. The coffin was open and the bloated face of Harry Binns lay on a pillow, darkly purple against the white satin.

'I figure he's holed up someplace in Foothills,' Lovell said with conviction. 'He wouldn't have chanced this country on foot.'

'Maybe,' Bishop allowed.

Lovell stared across at the lighted windows of the hotel. 'We look again,' he said at length, after long moments in which he smoked in silence. 'You start from here and take the west side. I'll go through to the other end. Reckon I'll try the cat house first. He might have doubled back there.'

'Okay, if that's what you want to do,' Bishop said.

'One thing,' Lovell said curtly, tossing away the half-smoked cigarette and catching hold of Bishop's shirt sleeve.

'Yeah?'

'You get him, you hold him. Or you shoot him in the leg or some other place that won't kill him. I want that bastard alive.'

Bishop jerked out of the other man's grip, and turned to face him squarely. 'That's the way I aim to get Adam, too,' he answered, returning Lovell's unwavering stare. 'And I aim to keep him alive to stand trial.'

Anger had driven the young deputy into revealing his intention. He waited for the city detective to react violently to the statement. Instead, Lovell merely smiled thinly and stepped down from the sidewalk.

'Man wants something as bad as you do, I reckon he's willing to fight for it,' he called back as he headed towards the Foothills Hotel.

'Whenever you're ready,' Bishop tossed after the retreating figure of the man. He let his hands drop to his sides, then tensed them, fingers curled to snap out his guns.

Lovell halted abruptly, but did not turn around. A girl laughed somewhere in the hotel and to Bishop it sounded like a derisive taunt. But it was from a different world and he did not allow it to disturb his concentration upon the unmoving form of Lovell.

Then the detective exploded a laugh of his own, and started again on his walk to the hotel. 'Not now or here, son,' he called without turning around. 'Another time and another place.'

Bishop relaxed with a sigh, recalling that these were the precise words used by the man Lovell was hunting. Lovell went through the doorway into the hotel lobby. Bishop stepped down from the sidewalk and dragged his feet wearily across the tracks made by the hearse.

Steele sat up in the rear of the hearse and stretched cramped muscles, then looked over the side of the casket at the dead, waxy features of Harry Binns. A sadness showed in his dark eyes for a moment, then was gone. He reached out of the open rear of the hearse, slid his rifle on the roof, then hauled himself up after it. As he dropped down on to the seat beside the driver, Jennie turned to look at him, her frightened face very white against the black hood.

'What you gonna do with me, mister?' she asked in a trembling voice as he plucked the reins from her hands.

'You turned me into a murderer, you know that?' he said, staring hard along the trail, which began to cant upwards towards a low ridge.

'You told me often enough,' the girl complained. 'I didn't know you were going to kill Binns.'

Steele nodded. 'That's why you're still in one piece,' he replied. 'And you being on such intimate terms with the undertaker is double insurance.'

Jennie's expression brightened with a hopeful smile. 'You're just gonna let me go?'

Steele shrugged, hauling hard on the reins as the hearse crested the ridge and he saw the farmstead nestling in the shallow valley below. 'Can't hurt a woman for lying,' he said. 'Just comes natural to them. So I'm just going to forget you, I hope.' He looked at her, and saw the relief in her face. 'All right, you can leave now.'

Her eyes flared angrily. 'You could have let me off sooner,' she accused. 'It's a long walk back to Foothills.'

Steele's mouth took a wry twist. 'You can use the time to reflect on the penalties of being a natural born woman.'

Jennie's movements were fast and angry as she climbed down from the hearse she had inveigled from the nervous mortician. 'I hope you get yours, mister!' she rasped at Steele.

He touched his hat brim. 'I always get what I want, lady,' he said, clucking to the horses.

They moved forward, hauling the hearse over the ridge and down the trail towards the farmstead. Jeannie watched its progress for awhile, then gave a toss of her head and whirled to face the long trek back to Foothills.

Again, there was just the one lighted window in the delapidated house. But as Steele rolled the hearse to a gentle halt in the yard, the door was flung open and Mona was silhouetted against the lamp light, the shotgun aimed from her shoulder. Steele sat, unmoving, on the seat, and saw the lines of hate etched into the woman's face.

'I picked up a rumour of the way it was between you and your brother-in-law, ma'am,' he said gently, implying no criticism. 'Least I could do was return him to his loved one.'

Mona squeezed both triggers at once, sending a double load of buckshot towards the hearse. The recoil flung her back into the house and she broke into sobs as she dropped the gun and slammed the door.

Steele ducked and snapped his head around as the glass side of the hearse was shattered into a million fragments. Shards of glass, buckshot and wood splinters tore into the dead flesh of the cadaver's face, erasing it completely. A single unmarked eye looked back at Steele from an unmoving sea of cold blood.

Up on the ridge trail, Jennie muttered: 'I hope you got yours,' and started to run in the direction of Foothills.

Steele leapt down from the shattered hearse, then his movements became casual as he strolled towards the closed door of the house. He tried the handle, but the lock had been turned. He raised the Colt Hartford and pumped two shells into the lock. Then he kicked the door wide and stepped across the threshold.

He was in a meagrely furnished living room, singularly lacking in the luxuries of life. There was a roughly made table surrounded by four odd chairs, sacking nailed up at the windows and a lopsided dresser with chipped and cracked crockery on its shelves. On the crude mantel above the ash-littered fireplace there were two matching vases and a pile of three books. Three pictures decorated the walls – one a woodcut of Jefferson Davis clipped from a magazine, a second done in pen and ink and showing Mona and Edward Binns at their wedding, and a third a photograph of Harry Binns outside his store.

Two doors led off to other rooms in the house and behind one of these, Mona was giving vent to her grief in the form of body-wrenching sobs. Steele back-heeled the front door closed and leaned against it, looking towards the source of the only noise in the house.

'I need some information, Mrs. Binns,' he called.

The woman's sobbing became more intense, interlaced with wails. Steele glanced around the room, then his blank eyes settled on one of the vases. He reached the mantel in three long strides and picked up the vase. It was either new, or had been lovingly cared for. It's finely-cut facets reflected the light from the kerosene lamp.

'The vases look like crystal, ma'am,' he said. 'You want to keep them?'

The woman did not interrupt her sobs for Harry Binns.

Steele sighed. 'Guess you don't.' He hurled the vase across the room. It hit the opposite wall and shattered. The sound silenced the woman. Steele listened for a few moments, then rested the rifle barrel on the mantel. 'One of a pair's no use keeping,' he said, and jerked the rifle.

The second vase toppled over the edge and was smashed to smithereens in the hearth. Mona began to wail again.

'Now for the books,' Steele called, picking them up and glancing at the titles. 'Hard to come by out here. Well-thumbed. You must enjoy reading them.'

'Do whatever you like, you . . . '. Mona could think of no epithet strong enough to describe her feelings towards the man who killed her lover.

Steele shrugged and crouched down in the hearth. He opened the books so that the pages flicked loosely in a chimney draught. Then he struck a match and set light to them. He watched them blaze, the firelight reflected in his eyes as in blank mirrors. After a few moments, he turned around on his haunches, decided on the picture of the former president of the Confederate States and crossed to rip it from the wall. He fed it to the fire and the flames consumed it eagerly.

'That was Davis just went up in smoke,' he explained. 'I guess it belonged to your husband. Your wedding picture goes next.'

He took the picture down and looked hard at it, familiarising himself with the lines of Ed Binns' unintelligent features. He decided Ed looked most unlike his brother, even when Harry was alive.

'All you have to do is come out here and talk to me,' he called, holding the picture above the flames, watching the stiff paper curl in the heat, listening for a reaction from the far side of the door.

There was only silence now, for the woman had cried herself dry of tears. The picture fell from Steele's gloved hand and was turned brown, then black. It disappeared and Steele crossed the room once more, to take down the sepia-toned photograph of Harry Binns. He looked at it sadly, then turned to look at the door.

'It was a mistake getting rid of Harry, Mrs Binns,' he called. 'But it was easy. His likeness will be a whole lot easier to finish.'

Feet thudded to the floor and bedsprings creaked. A moment later, the door was jerked open and Mona was there, her face ravaged by tears as she glared at Steele.

'Leave me something of him,' she pleaded hoarsely.

'Where did they go?' he asked, sliding the photograph backwards and forwards between a finger and thumb.

Mona sagged against the door jamb, emotionally and physically drained. 'Up in the mountains. Fuller's Folly.'

Steele eyed her with curiosity as she advanced into the room, holding out her dirt-grimed hands for the photograph. 'What's that, and where?'

She sighed. 'A fort. Like a foreign castle. Forty miles up the trail. Built by some loco Englishman called Colonel Fuller.'

'Easy to find?'

A vestige of the old hatred for Steele gleamed in her eyes. 'I hope so, for you. They'll kill you for sure.'

Steele put the photograph in her splayed hands and she looked at it a moment before pressing it against her breasts, as if it was the man himself she held. 'Maybe,' he replied. 'Or I'll kill them. I won't ask you to wish me luck. Just tell me where there's a saddle.'

Mona seemed not to hear him, then blinked and nodded. 'In the barn, over to the side of the yard.'

'I'm grateful,' Steele said, moving to the door. He opened it and halted to look back over his shoulder at her. 'I'm sorry I killed Harry,' he said. 'Least I can do is help you bury him. He's outside in the hearse.'

Mona tried to raise saliva into her mouth, but could not create enough to spit at him. She treated him to a glare of naked hatred. 'I don't want anything from you, mister.'

'Guess I can understand that, Mrs Binns,' he replied softly, and stepped out into the warm night.

He found an old but serviceable saddle in the barn and dragged it outside. Mona was at the end of the building, thrusting a spade into the ground. Steele recalled what hard work it had been to dig a grave for his father.

He unhitched the strongest looking horse from the hearse and saddled him. The woman continued to dig the grave without respite.

'Why did you marry the wrong brother, Mrs Binns?' he asked when he was mounted.

She flicked matted hair out of her eyes and stopped digging for a moment. 'Everyone makes mistakes, mister. I know you made at least one.'

'Yeah,' Steele agreed. 'And plenty more, I guess.'

Mona's tone became spiteful. 'But never one as big as your Ma and Pa.'

In the instant she spoke the last word, Steele came close to raising the presentation rifle and killing the woman. But then reason prevailed and he made allowances for her state of mind.

'It's conceivable,' he said, wheeled the horse and heeled it into a fast gallop out of the yard.

CHAPTER THIRTEEN

JENNIE had covered almost half the distance back to Foothills when she heard two riders galloping towards her. It was a warm night and even though she had taken off the heavy hooded cloak, she was sweating freely. But she would not admit to herself that the greater cause of her discomfort was fear rather than exertion – and she continually rebuked her imagination for conjuring up wraithlike movements among the timber and rock outcrops flanking the trail.

It was not quite so frightening when the trail cut across a flat, featureless area on which her own shadow was the only splash of black against black. But immediately she heard the distant clatter of hooves the fear returned – and was increased by the knowledge that she had nowhere to hide. All she could do was stop and peer ahead into the night, hoping she knew the riders: or that they were strangers who meant her no harm.

For a long time after they crested a rise and rode hard towards her they were merely dark silhouettes. She chewed hard on her lip and the cloak became crumpled and damp with sweat as she kneaded the material with her hands. Then moonlight struck a star and the pent-up breath sighed from her lungs.

'Lawmen, for Christ sake!' she gasped as Lovell and Bishop brought their mounts to a dust-raising halt in front of her. 'I thought for a while you were just more trouble.'

Lovell eyed her pretty face and slim body appraisingly. 'You in trouble then, Lady?' he asked coolly.

Jennie was apprehensive of his cruel eyes, but forced a grin to her features as she rubbed her flat stomach. 'Not that kind, mister, He had other things on his mind.'

'Like what?' Lovell asked sourly.

The girl shot a glance at Bishop, much preferring his youthful good looks and the expression of mild curiosity which cloaked them. But the deputy offered no greeting. Jennie shrugged and returned her attention to the man in the frock coat.

'Lousy bastard made me drive him out to the Binns' place. On a hearse for Christ sake.'

Bishop shot a glance at Lovell, and saw the Washington detective slide hurriedly from his saddle. Jennie took a step backwards, but Lovell's long arms reached out and his hands clawed over her shoulders, fingernails digging hard into her flesh through the material of her dress.

'Who?'

Jennie winced. 'Who what?'

'Who did you drive out to the farm?' Lovell demanded.

'You're hurting me, mister,' Jennie complained.

Lovell shook the girl violently, rocking her head back and forth. 'Answer the question or you'll get hurt a lot worse.'

Tears squeezed out of Jennie's eyes. Up close, Lovell's face seemed to hold all the evil in the world. She swallowed hard and tried to speak, but Lovell shook her again, rattling her teeth together.

'Let her go, Lovell,' Bishop instructed softly.

Lovell froze for a split-second and from the stare he fixed upon Jennie's face, she was certain he was going to kill her. But suddenly he hurled her away from him. She stumbled backwards and fell hard to the ground. Lovell whirled, jerking the revolver from its holster. His murderous eyes locked upon Bishop's surprised eyes.

'You giving me orders, deputy?' the city detective demanded shrilly.

Bishop swallowed his shock, knowing that if he had made the mistake of pointing a gun at the man, Lovell would have shot him. 'I'm telling you to treat people decent,' he replied softly.

'Decent people get treated decently,' Lovell snarled. 'Any woman comes out here with a man ain't decent.'

Jennie clambered painfully to her feet. 'What you calling me, mister?' she shrieked. 'I didn't come out here because – '

Lovell showed his speed again, side-stepping and pivoting. The revolver swung and smashed viciously across Jennie's face. She fell again, a scream exploding from her throat as blood erupted from a long gash on her cheek. Bishop's right hand streaked for his gun, but he was not fast enough. He halted the movement abruptly as Lovell's revolver raked around to cover him again.

'Anyone stands in my way, he gets to lie down,' the Washington detective hissed. 'And not get up.'

For a sliver of time, it seemed as if the young deputy intended to complete the act of drawing. Lovell's eyes were blazing with fury and his knuckle was white around the trigger. Then the tension drained out of Bishop. He swung a leg over his saddle and dropped to the ground. Lovell's expression became scornful as he watched the deputy move towards the injured girl, then stoop and help her up into a sitting position.

Jennie sobbed and the fear was bright behind her tears as she looked across at Lovell. 'What he do that for?'

'He just likes hurting things,' Bishop replied softly, grimacing as he saw the jagged flesh of the wound. 'What was the name of the man you took out to the Binns place, miss?'

'He said it was Steele,' she replied, and looked again at Lovell as the detective made a sound of anger deep in his throat. 'I think he killed Mrs Binns. Or she killed him – I should be so lucky to have my wishes come true.'

Lovell slid the gun back into his stomach holster and swung up into the saddle. Bishop allowed Jennie's trembling form to rest back on the ground again. Then he stood up and mounted.

'Apologies, miss,' he said. 'We'd escort you back to town, but we got things to do.'

Lovell wheeled his horse first, and galloped away. Bishop touched his hat and took off in pursuit. Jennie struggled to her feet and used the sleeve of her dress to wipe the blood from her cheek.

'There's just no gentlemen left in the lousy world,' she muttered angrily, then turned and continued the long trek back to town.

Light still spilled from the open doorway of the rundown house in the valley, not extending to the open grave at the end of the bullet-splintered barn. But there was enough moonlight to show up the rectangular pit and mound of fresh earth beside it.

Mona emerged from the house, the shotgun cradled in the crook of her arm, and moved wearily towards the new grave. Her gait was slow, but when she heard distant hoofbeats, she lengthened her stride. She halted at the lip of the pit and discovered fresh tears to squeeze from her red-rimmed eyes as she stared down at the casket containing the body of her lover.

She continued to stand in the same manner for a long time, until Lovell and Bishop galloped their lathered mounts into the yard. Then she made a sudden movement and the shotgun discharged both its barrels. The lawmen struggled to calm their rearing animals.

Mona's body crumpled over the edge of the grave and thudded on to the lid of the casket. There was a massive crater where her breast had once been. Blood bubbled up to fill it, then overflowed the sides. The shotgun stock splashed into the pool of thick, scarlet liquid.

The two lawmen brought their horses under control and walked the nervous animals over to the edge of the grave. They looked down at the ghastly sight, Lovell dispassionately, Bishop with horror.

'They reckoned she was pretty cosy with her brother-in-law,' Lovell said.

'A man like you wouldn't understand a love like that,' Bishop rasped, turning away from the gruesome mutilation of the dead woman.

'I understand something about this,' Lovell muttered.

'What's that?'

'It's one more death Adam Steele has to answer for,' Lovell snarled, his eyes raking the surface of the yard. 'Hey . . . there's some horse tracks over there.'

He led the way to the corner of the house.

'You're not wrong,' Bishop said wryly.

'Looks like there was a stampede through here,' Lovell mused, his cruel eyes rising from the churned-up ground to peer across the pastureland spreading westwards from the rear of the house.

'Horse soldiers, Lovell,' Bishop explained. 'It's not only Adam and us playing tag out here.'

Lovell stared at the deputy suspiciously. 'What do you know I don't?' he demanded.

'What I found out by using my tongue instead of my gun,' Bishop replied, and this time it was he who was first to heel his horse forward, chasing out over the upgrade of the valley side.

Lovell's features formed into a sneer as he set off in pursuit.

CHAPTER FOURTEEN

ED Binns yawned, then grimaced as he swept his dull eyes over the sleeping forms of his three partners. He stood up and stretched his arms above his head, seeking to ease the ache in his muscles. Then he glanced over the campsite and the surrounding terrain, the whole bathed in blue-tinted moonlight. Carstairs, Logan and Monahan slept, fully dressed, on the grassy bank of a fast-flowing stream. Binns' sentry position was in the shadows of an ancient silver birch tree with gnarled branches spreading out in every direction. The horses were ground hobbled on the far side of the camp, ready saddled in case a fast getaway was forced upon the wanted men.

To the north, on the other side of the stream, the country fell away in a series of broken steps almost denuded of vegetation until it levelled out into a vast expanse of forest. In all other directions, the terrain was gently undulating, carpeted with lush grass and featured here and there stands of timber or clumps of thick brush.

It was from a stand of mixed timber that Lieutenant Carey and the troopers under his command watched the actions of the bored sentry. They saw him make a circuit of the camp, scratching his armpit as he dragged his feet. Then they watched as he halted and pulled a watch from his vest pocket. They were too far away to see the smile of relief which spread across his unintelligent features.

Adam Steele, his face and clothes dripping with water, was close enough to see Binns' pleasure that his stint of guard duty was over. He was crouched among the reeds under the bank of the stream, his body braced against the tug of the rushing water, the Colt Hartford resting across his shoulder well clear of the surface. He had waded across, and taken up his position beneath the overhanging branches of the birch, while Binns was making his inspection tour of the camp.

Now he heard the whispered conversation of the men.

'Snap out of it, Jack,' Binns hissed. 'Your turn.'

Logan groaned, sat up suddenly and raised his wooden club. Then he recognised Binns and groaned again. 'All quiet?'

' 'Cepting for the frigging river,' Binns muttered, flopping down on to the blanket still warm from Logan's body.

Logan stood up, tugging at the crotch of his pants, and glanced distastefully at the white water of the stream. 'Crazy idea,' he complained to himself as he ambled over to the tree and sat down, leaning his back against the trunk. 'Ain't nobody but us in this neck of the woods.'

He didn't sound convinced of the fact, and clutched the club in both hands across his bulbous stomach. After a minute or so, his eyelids began to droop.

Steele snaked his body up on to the bank of the stream, the rush of water masking any slight sound he made. He glanced up at the sky and gave a small nod of satisfaction as he saw scattered clouds scudding together to form a heavy bank in the west. The star-dotted area between the leading edge of the cloud and the bright near-sphere of the moon narrowed as he watched.

Lieutenant Carey was also watching the sky, viewing it through a tracery of leaves at the edge of the timber.

'We going to go and get them, sir?' the sergeant whispered, leaning forward to stroke the nose of his horse.

'Now's as good a time as any, I think,' Carey replied, dropping his gaze to the campsite at the foot of the slope, some three hundred feet away. 'Be pitch black before long – hey, what's that?'

The sergeant, and those troopers who had a view of the camp, craned forward to see what had caught the lieutenant's attention.

Steele had raised himself on to all fours, then into a stooped shoulders crouch. He moved forward on a curved course, putting the trunk of the tree between himself and the dozing Logan. At the tree, he straightened and side-stepped around it. Logan sensed, rather than heard, the intruder. He opened his eyes wide and looked up, his mouth dropping open to shout a warning to the others. But the rifle was already flashing down towards him. Steele abruptly changed the direction of the blow and the barrel lashed across Logan's exposed throat. A low gasp erupted from the man. Then his head smashed back against the tree trunk and he slumped forward into unconsciousness.

Steele grasped one limp arm and dragged Logan's unresponsive form towards the bank of the stream.

It was this act which Carey saw, and he continued to watch in stunned silence for another few moments, until Steele and his prisoner disappeared over the bank. Then he quickly turned his head around to stare at the sergeant, and jerked his rifle from the saddle boot.

'Let's go, for Christ sake!' he rasped, thudding his heels into the flanks of his horse.

He burst clear of the trees and the troopers needed no order from the sergeant to follow him. The downward slope gave added impetus to the charge and it was the vibrations of the ground under the thundering hoofbeats, rather than the sound, which roused the sleeping men.

'It's the frigging army again!' Binns yelled, leaping to his feet and grabbing his rifle as he stared in awe at the troopers streaming towards the camp.

'Stay and watch if you like!' Monahan rasped, springing up, rifle in hand, and racing in pursuit of Carstairs, who was first to swing up into his saddle.

'Where the hell's Logan?' Binns roared, breaking into a run that was fast enough to overhaul Monahan.

'More pressing problems, old son,' Carstairs replied, ducking as the charging troopers sent a volley of shots high over the campsite. His heels dug hard into the flanks of his mount and the animal snorted and flung itself into a full gallop from a standing start.

He snapped out a revolver and fired over his shoulder. Binns and Monahan swung into their saddles at the same time, held back a second to fire at the soldiers, then galloped off in the wake of the Englishman.

The corporal cartwheeled from his horse, blood pumping from his throat. A trooper watched the flailing arms and legs of the dead man in horror, then snarled and sent a bullet low towards the trio ahead. It bit a fragment of flesh out of Binns' right ear and the injured man shouted aloud, more from surprise than pain.

'High, for effect!' Carey raged. 'We need them alive.'

'What about the other one, sir?' the sergeant asked breathlessly, veering his horse in close to the galloping mount of the angry lieutenant.

'Later, sergeant!' Carey snapped, trying to urge more speed from his horse as the wanted men were lost to sight over the crest of a low hillock.

On the far side of the rise, Carstairs led Monahan and Binns diagonally down a gentle slope and into a gully with sheer sides and a rocky bed. The hoofbeats of their horses resounded tumultuously, directing the troopers towards the mouth of the gully even though they could not see their quarry.

The gully cut a tortuous course through the centre of a hill, then widened out into a broad ravine with many other gullies leading off it. The ground underfoot was uneven, scattered with small rocks and larger boulders left by some primeval natural upheaval. The three men left no tracks as they turned sharply into one of the side gullies. And suddenly, as if their horses had spread wings and soared into thin air, the sound of the hoofbeats ceased.

So that when Carey burst out into the ravine he was greeted by an empty silence. Conscious of the danger to horses and men from the scattered rocks in addition to bullets from sharpshooters firing from cover, he signalled a halt.

'Looks like we lost them, sir,' the sergeant said, spitting.

'Men just don't disappear, sergeant!' Carey snapped, raking his eyes over the many escape routes from the ravines. 'Good chance a lot of these clefts are dead ends. Split the men into groups of four. Move slow and easy – and I want at least one of those civilians left alive.'

A slow grin spread across the red face of the non-com. And there was a muttering of approval from the troopers as they divided themselves into groups. The lieutenant had changed the orders – offering his men the chance to kill two of the fugitives. They turned their mounts towards the gully entrances, rifles cocked and ready to spit death.

It was Carey himself, riding slightly ahead of three troopers, who entered the cleft into which the quarry had disappeared. But neither the officer nor the enlisted men noted that one of the patches of heavy shadow against the rock face was, in fact, the mouth of a cave. Deep inside this, Binns made soft cooing noises to the horses as Carstairs and Monahan crouched down in front of him, sighting their rifles out into the gully.

The horse soldiers clattered by and Monahan let out pent-up

breath in a soft sigh. Carstairs' eyes glinted at him warningly. Monahan grimaced and resumed his concentration across the cave. Less than a minute had gone by before the four blue uniformed men rode back the way they had come. Carey's voice floated into the cave, the confined space giving it a ghostly tone.

'Let's hope the bastards rode into one as short as this,' he said. 'There's just no way out.'

Carstairs continued to aim towards the opening for as long as he could hear the thud of hooves against rock. Then he swung back on his haunches, rested his rifle on the ground and sat down. His teeth gleamed in a self-satisfied smirk as he looked at the others.

'What you reckon happened to Logan, Bill?' Binns asked, continuing to caress each horse in turn.

'Perhaps he had to piss at the wrong time, old son,' the Englishman replied, stretching out on the damp ground.

Monahan relaxed, resting his back against the cave wall. 'Probably spotted the damn army and took it on the lam without warning us, the crud,' he said, disgruntled.

Binns considered both answers for a few moments. Then: 'How long we gonna hole up in this place?' he asked.

Carstairs' voice was sleepy. 'I saw one of them go down. Before long, I think a detail of the troop will double back to check on him. After that, we can move out. Until then, I intend to catch up on my sleep which was so rudely interrupted.'

'Who's gonna keep watch?' Binns asked.

Monahan's chin was resting on his chest and he gave a low snore.

Carstairs yawned. 'Frank seems to be asleep already, old son. Wake us if you see anything out there.'

Binns flung down the reins of the horses, snatched the rifle from his saddle boot and ambled reluctantly towards the mouth of the cave. It's Logan's turn, goddamnit!' he growled.

'Logan is apparently otherwise engaged, old son,' Carstairs pointed out drowsily.

Binns spat out of the cave mouth. It hit the rock as just another spot of moisture, for the cloud bank had now completely covered the sky and begun to drop the first wet promises of a downpour.

It was also raining on the dead corporal slumped on the slope above the campsite; on the mounted figure of Adam Steele; and the helpless form of Jack Logan.

Steele had used the lariat from Logan's own saddle to bind the unconscious man, tying his arms close to his sides and clamping his legs together at the knees and ankles. Logan remained unconscious as Steele used the remainder of the rope to suspend his prisoner, upside-down, from a branch of the tree extending out over the rushing stream.

The rain was moving in from the west – the direction from which the stream ran – and Steele adjusted the ropc so that Logan's head was only some six inches above the white water. Then, his heavily stubbed face set in an expression of indifferent detachment, he retrieved his horse and mounted. He sat patiently, waiting for Logan to return to his full senses, and watching as the level of the water rose at least two inches. It was cold spume lashing against his face which accelerated Logan's plunge into horrified awareness. His eyes bulged from his blood red face as he stared across the angry water towards Steele. The rain came down harder, driven by a keen wind.

Logan opened his mouth to plead for mercy, but a distant thunderclap masked his words. Steele waited for the sound to die away. But he had to raise his voice to be heard above the spatter of rain and roar of rushing water.

'Sorry I can't hang around with you,' he said coldly. 'But this animal is a little skittish. Best to get him out of the area before the storm breaks.'

He jerked on the reins, turning the animal towards the west, then heeled him forward. He heard the start of Logan's terrified scream, but another crash of thunder blanketed the sound. The horse leapt forward into a gallop.

Logan snapped his mouth tight closed as water splashed into it.

CHAPTER FIFTEEN

HIGH in the mountains, at almost noon the next day, the storm had been and gone. It had left many pools of clear, cool water behind it and at one of these, Carstairs called a halt so that men and horses could drink. It was a welcome rest, for the sky had been clear since shortly after dawn and the sun seemed to blaze down with renewed intensity, as if resenting the cooling relief provided by the night's rain.

'Damn funny that lieutenant didn't send back men to check on his wounded,' Carstairs muttered, lighting a ready-made cigarette.

It was the first thing anybody had said for a long time. Carstairs had been morose ever since he woke, giving the impression that he did not believe Binns' report that the night had passed quietly. He had implied, without putting the accusation into words, that Binns had slept during his guard duty and thus had failed to note the troopers' movements.

Binns, after an initial angry outburst, had slumped into a resentful silence.

Monahan was not, by nature, a garrulous man.

'Shows you can't be right every time, Bill,' Binns replied, with ill-concealed spite.

Monahan finished drinking from his hat, then poured water over his head. 'All it shows is that the army's in a hurry,' he said sourly.

Carstairs blew out a stream of smoke, then fixed Binns with a cold stare. 'My line of thought precisely, Frank, old son,' he said softly.

Binns unlocked his eyes from the stare, only to find that Monahan was watching him with the same degree of coldness. 'What you looking at me for?' he demanded.

Carstairs' voice became larded with soft menace. 'How much did your wife know about Colonel Fuller and the plan, Ed?' he asked.

'Nothing,' Binns shot back, licking his lips.

'I find that difficult to believe,' Carstairs said in a the same tone. 'Ever since we left the cave, we've been following the sign left by those troopers.'

Monahan nodded. 'And they're heading straight up towards the fort.'

Binns swallowed hard. 'Even if she knew, she wouldn't say anything. She'd know what I'd do to her.'

Carstairs dropped his cigarette. Monahan stomped on it, then turned towards Binns. The latter cowered away before Monahan's threatening expression and stance.

'You got a big mouth, Ed,' Monahan accused. 'Maybe something ought to be done about it.'

Carstairs raised a restraining hand. 'Frank!' he barked. 'If he's spoken out of turn, the colonel will punish him.' A smile spread across his handsome features. 'You know what interesting methods of punishment he devises.'

Monahan turned away from the trembling Binns and gave a short, harsh laugh. 'Yeah, that's right, Bill,' he agreed.

'I didn't,' Binns blubbered. 'I didn't say nothing to Mona. The army don't know where it's goin'. Likely they'll go off at a wrong turn someplace ahead.'

'Pray that they do, Ed, old son,' Carstairs urged. 'There isn't anybody so inventive as Colonel Fuller when it comes to making wrongdoers suffer.'

'We moving out now?' Monahan asked.

Carstairs nodded, then swung up into the saddle. I think so. If the army should find the fort, I'd hate to miss their welcome. I haven't fought a battle proper since the colonel and I left India.'

'With your friends?' Monahan said slyly, as he slid a foot into the saddle stirrup and swung himself upwards.

'What friends?' Binns asked, half-curious, half-nervous.

'If the army gets to reach the fort because of your big mouth, you'll get to meet them, Ed,' Monahan replied.

Binns blinked, then hurriedly mounted as the others set off.

He urged his horse into a canter to catch up with them, then slowed to match their walking pace.

On high ground ahead and to the left of the trio of riders, Adam Steele sighted down the length of the rifle barrel and drew a bead on the head of Carstairs. He was stretched out full length on sun-warmed ground, in the cover of a huge boulder, with a clear field of fire at the riders and the ground for five hundred feet in front of them.

He changed his aim to line up a shot on Binns, held it for a moment, then transferred his attention to Monahan. The only rider not in eastern garb had slowed and dropped behind the others, taking time to adjust the fancy California headstall of his mount.

Steele lined up a perfect shot at the nape of his target's neck, then abruptly lowered the rifle a fraction and squeezed tae trigger. He saw a gout of blood erupt from Monahan's leg, then the flop of the man as he went sideways from the saddle and crashed to the ground.

The loose horse streaked away and Steele swung the rifle, drawing a bead upon the ground between the horses of the other men. He sent three shots whining into the dirt in quick succession, causing both mounted horses to wheel and rear.

'Where the hell are they?' Binns yelled fearfully, trying to look around him and pin-point the sharpshooter as he struggled at the same time to bring his horse under control.

'If you want to stay and find out, you're welcome,' Carstairs shouted, heeling his horse into a gallop, backing up his demand with a heavy hand and high-pitched yell.

Steele fired more shots, careful not to hit the men or horses, then quickly reloaded the Colt Hartford.

'The bastards have doubled back!' Binns roared, urging his horse to chase in pursuit of Carstairs and the loose animal.

Steele sent a further burst of rapid fire after them, then ducked behind the cover of the rock as a bullet whistled over his head.

Carstairs and Binns rode out of sight, but he could still hear the thud of their horses' hooves to signal their continued retreat. Another shot sounded from below and he wriggled to the far side of the rock before chancing a furtive surveillance.

He saw a large patch of blood soaking into the dirt where Monahan had fallen. Then his impressive eyes followed a thin trail of red until it disappeared over the rim of a small depression. He was forced to duck back into cover as the injured man sent another shot whining up the slope towards his hiding place.

Far ahead, out of sight of the ambush, but within earshot of the gunfire, Carstairs and Binns slowed their sweating horses to a walk. They heard Steele's rifle explode two shots in answer to Monahan's one.

'He isn't giving up without a fight,' Binns said breathlessly.

'He's got nothing to lose, old son,' Carstairs pointed out. 'If they catch him, he'll hang.'

Binns blinked. 'The same goes for us, don't it?'

Carstairs gave a wry smile. 'I didn't think you'd want to go back to lend a hand, old son.'

'Let's go,' Binns said nervously. 'I won't feel safe until I'm in the fort. How far now?'

Carstairs waited until another burst of distant gunfire was over. 'Too far for comfort, I think.'

The horses, their weariness evident from flared nostrils, bulging eyes and the white lather on their flanks, were asked for more speed. It was not long before the two men had ridden out of earshot of the gunfire.

In fact, there were no other shots to hear. Monahan had rained a whole fusillade of bullets against Steele's covering rock, while Steele had pressed himself against the ground and reloaded. Then a silence which seemed to stretch seconds into minutes hovered in the hot air above the slope. It was broken by Monahan's voice, the words twisted by pain.

'Okay, up there! Okay! I'm beat. Out of shells and bleeding like a stuck pig. You win, soldier boy.'

Steele stayed in cover. 'Get on your feet and come out with your hands up,' he yelled.

'How the frigging hell can I?' Monahan snarled. 'You shot half my leg off.'

'So, crawl into the open,' Steele shouted in reply, and peered around the side of the rock.

Monahan, his tanned face contorted by the agony of his leg, clawed his way up out of the dip. Steele could see that he still wore his gunbelt, but the double holsters were empty. He raised himself, turned and ambled up the slope, unhitching his horse from the far side of a patch of high brush. He mounted and rode back down the slope.

The injured man was sprawled, flat on his stomach, one hand retaining a vice-like grip on his leg wound, the other trapped beneath his chest. Steele had slid the rifle into its boot, but his hand swung loosely at his side, close to the slit in his pants' seam.

'Man that's unconscious wouldn't have a grip like that,' Steele said softly.

Despite his pain, Monahan was able to move with smooth speed. Even as Steele spoke the final word, the man on the ground lunged into a half roll, flinging himself on to his back. The hand which had been beneath his body pumped up, as if on a spring, and one of the revolvers drew an inverted bead on Steele.

Steele was a fraction faster, his hand plunging through the slit seam, streaking out and arcing forward. Sunlight glinted on the spinning blade. Monahan screamed and the revolver exploded into sound.

The bullet went wide, fired from a gun sailing through the air. Monahan stared in agonised horror at the knife blade, which had entered the back of his hand and penetrated between the bones to protrude through his palm. Whimpering sounds trickled from his mouth.

Steele dismounted and Monahan looked up as the shadow of his attacker fell across him.

'Do something!' Monahan begged, extending his hand with its ghastly, blood-dripping appendage.

Steele grasped Monahan's fingers in one gloved hand, then gripped the knife handle and jerked. Monahan emitted another high scream, then gagged as his own blood sprayed into his open mouth. Steele stooped, and wiped the knife blade on Monahan's shirt before replacing it in the boot sheath.

'You ain't army,' Monahan accused, his injured hand resting on his heaving chest as he clutched at his leg wound. 'Who the frigging hell are you?'

Steele unhitched the rope from the saddle he had taken from the Binns farm. 'An orphan,' he answered. 'Like you said awhile back, you're beat. I think you ought to keep laying down.'

'No!' Monahan screamed as Steele bent over him.

'Guess that's what my father told you,' Steele said. 'You should have listened.'

It took almost fifteen minutes to strip the weakly struggling Monahan, then stake him out, using lengths of ropes and pegs ready cut for the purpose. The sun had exceeded its noon peak by then, but the cloudless sky promised many hours of blazing heat still to come. A swarm of flies, which had buzzed impatiently while Steele worked on his whimpering victim, zoomed in and split into two groups as he backed away and swung into the saddle.

They gorged avidly on the blood of the open wounds.

Monahan made a final effort to break free of the ropes holding his legs splayed and his arms wide. It drained him of his last reserves of strength. Even the hate which brimmed in his eyes lacked vigor as he stared up at his torturer.

'Rest easy – and long,' Steele said in farewell, as he wheeled his horse and rode off towards the distant mountain peaks.

CHAPTER SIXTEEN

LATE in the afternoon, on a small, rocky plateau in the high country, Lieutenant Carey halted the troop and the men ate a meagre meal washed down with strong coffee. They were weary and their tiredness was compounded by the frustration of the knowledge that they were probably wasting their time and energy.

There was little conversation during the meal, and afterwards, it was the red-faced sergeant who voiced the men's feelings to the officer.

'Bad country to track in, Lieutenant,' he said, flopping down beside Carey in the shade of a low bluff. 'Man nor beast leave much sign on this stuff.'

He thudded his heel against the solid rock of the ground. On the far side of the campsite, the horses stamped their feet, as if in agreement. There were a few patches of tough grass on which to feed, but it was poor eating.

Carey sighed and rubbed his stubbled jaw. 'I'm too tired to listen to the obvious, sergeant,' he replied disconsolately. 'They could have holed up and waited for us to pass, or they could have gone off at a tangent we missed. Unless you have something constructive to say, leave me alone to think.'

The sergeant cleared his throat. 'I have only one thing to say, sir.'

Carey detected an inflection in the other's tone which captured his waning attention. 'What's that, sergeant?' he asked.

'Begging the lieutenant's pardon, but I think we should have sent a man back to check on Corporal Reagan, sir.'

Carey seemed about to rebuke the non-com for the criticism,

but then let his anger escape in a sigh. 'Reagan poured his life out through his throat,' he said softly. 'He's dead, and he was the fifth man we lost. And two more deserted. I can't spare anybody for a useless errand.'

'We might have captured the fourth conspirator, sir,' the sergeant insisted.

Carey's irritation grew again. 'A decoy,' he shot back curtly. 'We were expected to follow him and be thrown off the track. We can't afford to foul up this mission, sergeant. It's of the utmost urgency and importance.'

The veteran non-com shrugged. 'I ain't an officer, sir. I don't get confided in.'

'And you're not about to be,' Carey replied with a note of finality. 'So get some rest so you'll be fresh to start the search again.'

Carey allowed his chin to fall to his chest. The sergeant sighed and stretched out full length on the ground. The enlisted men adopted whatever posture they found most comfortable on the hard, uneven ground. No sentries were posted since, Carey reasoned, they were the hunters and had nothing to fear from the hunted.

He was wrong.

Carstairs and Binns had moved up close to the campsite while the troopers were still eating. Binns had been anxious to circle the plateau and ride hard for Fuller's Folly, but Carstairs had insisted they keep watch for awhile.

Now, as he watched the soldiers take their rest, the Englishman smiled with satisfaction that his decision had been proved the right one. 'Cover me,' he muttered, sinking to the ground and bellying forward, keeping down below the scattering of rocks between Binns' hiding place and the patch of shade where the horses were tethered.

Binns opened his mouth to protest, but Carstairs was already gone. He rested both rifle barrels on the rock and struggled to keep his hands from trembling as he hooked fingers around each trigger. His eyes flicked back and forth between the sleeping soldiers and the group of horses. One or two troopers moved in their sleep: others grunted or snored. The horses whinnied as Carstairs moved in among them. The blade of his knife glinted occasionally as he sawed through the tethers.

It was less than a minute later that the Englishman returned to pluck his rifle from Binns' nervous grasp. '*Come on,*' he mouthed, and led the way up sloping ground to a grotesquely formed outcrop.

Their horses waited behind the rock formation and Binns was shaking so much it took him many fumbling seconds to mount.

'We going now?' he asked, wiping sweat from his eyes.

Carstairs' handsome face wore a contemptuous frown, but then he smiled. 'Like bats out of hell,' he said, and heeled his mount forward, controlling the animal with his knees as he grasped his rifle in both hands.

Binns stared at the Englishman in numb shock, hardly able to believe the evidence of his own eyes as he saw him racing down towards the campsite.

'You're crazy!' Binns yelled as the Englishman squeezed off his first shot. But the company of a madman was preferable to being stranded alone in country thick with army troopers. Binns galloped in the wake of Carstairs, drawing a Remington from under his suit jacket.

A cry of pain and shouts of alarm rose from the troopers as the first shot resounded among the high peaks. Panicked horses, finding themselves free, wheeled, reared and bolted. The first man to be hit spilled blood from his stomach. The flying hoof of a loose horse crashed against a soldier's head and the man's neck snapped like dried timber.

Another trooper scooped up a rifle and squeezed off a shot. Binns' derby skimmed from his head. The Tennessee farmer squealed in fear and fired wildly. The man with the rifle spun away, taking the bullet in his shoulder. A string of three loose horses galloped over him, trampling his head to a bubbling red pulp.

The sergeant grabbed at the cut tether of a horse and was dragged several yards before he was forced to release the animal. The tattered remnants of his uniform breeches were stained bright red with blood drawn by jagged rock scraping through skin.

Carey went down on to one knee and sighted at the zigzagging figure of Carstairs. He squeezed the trigger, but at that instant a freed horse swerved in front of him. The animal took the bullet in the brain and rolled over. A young trooper screamed and fainted as the tremendous dead weight collapsed across his lower legs, crushing them and bursting open the flesh.

Such was Binns' fear, he drew level with Carstairs, lashing at his horse unmercifully to urge the animal to the limit of its speed.

They rode clear of the campsite on the far side, flanked by half a dozen of the loose army horses.

'Some reveille, eh?' Carstairs shouted with a laugh, then ducked low as a fusillade of shots exploded behind him and bullets whined about him.

Binns could not reply. His mouth was full of vomit, which erupted and streamed out behind him as he rode.

Carey squeezed off two final shots, then hurled his empty rifle away. 'All right!' he roared, staring after the distance-shrinking figures of Carstairs and Binns. 'Cease fire.' The screams of the wounded and the anger pounding in the ears of the soldiers who were unscathed, prevented them hearing the officer's order. Carey whirled around and cupped his hands to his mouth. His voice became a bellow: 'Cease fire, I said! There's nothing to hit!'

Lead continued to pour after the attackers for several seconds; and it was the fact that they rode from sight, rather than in compliance with Carey's order, which persuaded the troopers of the futility of further retaliation.

Carey's anger became disgust for a moment, as he surveyed the dead, dying and wounded. But an inward-directed rage powered his voice as he felt the eyes of the men upon him. 'Catch the damn horses, for Christ sake!' he snarled.

On a hill crest high above the blood-run plateau, Adam Steele stroked the neck of his horse and shook his head. 'Makes you wonder how the Union won the war with officers like that,' he muttered.

Then he clucked to the animal and urged him forward, turning his eyes away from the body-littered scene below, towards the distant dots of movement which were Carstairs and Binns.

In what remained of daylight, Steele narrowed the gap between himself and the two men ahead of him. By dusk he was less than a quarter of a mile behind them. When full night was born, he was close enough to hear their intermittent conversation as a low, unintelligible murmuring.

When they entered an abandoned line-shack after putting their horses in a stable at the back, he was close enough to see them – and to recognise Ed Binns from the wedding picture he had burned at the farmstead.

Steele's vantage point was a small stand of pine trees slightly to the side and some twenty yards in front of the shack. The building was single storey, with no glass in the windows on each side of the leaning door. There was a large hole in the sloping roof. Moonlight shafted in through the opening. Steele's eyes were expressionless as he dismounted and peered across at the shack, seeing clearly the forms of Carstairs and Binns, one at each window. Their whispered conversation was amplified by the stillness of the night.

'You sure it was just the one horse you heard, Bill?'

'Yes, old son. Of course, it may have been a loose one.'

'He sure followed us a long way.'

Carstairs tone became pensive. 'That's what worries me.'

As he listened, Steele unbuckled the cinch and slid the saddle silently from the back of his horse. He lowered it to the ground and drew the Colt Hartford from the boot. Then he jabbed the rifle muzzle hard into the animal's rump.

The horse snorted and lunged clear of the pines, galloping across the front of the shack. Binns gave a cry of alarm and fired through the glassless window, missing the pained animal. Carstairs took more careful aim. Binns fired again. The horse took both bullets in the shoulder and staggered. Carstairs squeezed off a second shot, hitting the animal's head. It sighed into death and keeled over.

Steele completed his run and pressed himself against the side of the shack, holding his breath in lungs which seemed ready to burst.

'It *was* just a loose one, Bill.'

'Perhaps, old son,' the Englishman replied thoughtfully. 'But what made him come out of those trees as if somebody had jabbed him?'

'You think – ' Binns voice had taken on a tremulous tone.

'Lately, I've learned to take nothing for granted. Take a look at the back.'

'Why don't we just make a run for it?' Binns demanded.

'Not until it's known to be safe,' Carstairs snapped. 'Just do as I say, there's a good fellow.'

Steele side-stepped towards the rear of the shack, then ran diagonally across the yard on the balls of his feet. When Binns creaked open the rear door and thrust his rifle out, then his head, the yard was empty. He snaked his body around the frame and pressed himself hard against the timber wall, eyes straining for the slighest movement, ears for the tiniest sound. Nothing moved. Some crickets chirped. Binns held his position for a full ten seconds, then: 'Ain't nothing out here, Bill.'

'Check the stable,' Carstairs replied.

His voice sounded further away than it should have been. But Binns realised his ears could be playing tricks on him, considering the strain he was under. He stepped away from the shack wall and moved slowly towards the gaping hole in the stable, where once a door had been. The ground crunched under his feet. The horses made small grunts. The crickets' excitement mounted. There was a faint swishing sound.

Binns screamed. He dropped the rifle and clutched at his shoulder. He felt the warmth of blood and the smooth roundness of the knife handle.

'Bill!' he screamed, dropping to his knees, half turning to look towards the shack, his hands fumbling to pull the knife from his flesh.

Footfalls sounded – running. They grew fainter, running away. There was a thud and Binns keeled over, full-length, turning his head to look towards the stable. Steele stood in the gaping doorway, legs still splayed and bent after his leap from the hayloft. The Colt Hartford was crooked in his arm. Binns gasped and streaked out a hand towards his discarded rifle. Steele snapped up the sporting gun to the aim and squeezed the trigger. The bullet smashed into the stock of Binns' Henry and the man snatched away his hand.

'Your shooting days are over, feller,' Steele said, approaching Binns slowly. 'Same as your lynching days – and every other kind.'

Confusion showed in Binns eyes, shining through tears of pain and fear. 'Bill?' he bellowed suddenly.

The footfalls had faded into the distance. The crickets and the horses were silent. The moonlit stillness had an eerie quality.

'Ran out on you,' Steele said. 'With the kind of friends you fellers pick, you don't deserve an enemy like me.'

He stooped, held Binns pinned to the ground with the rifle muzzle and jerked the knife free. Binns screamed, then watched in mute horror as Steele wiped the blade on his shirt.

'Who are you, mister?' he managed to gasp at length.

Steele's face, heavily bearded after many days without a shave, was menacing in its utter lack of any kind of expression. His voice was flat: 'To you – slow death.'

Once more, Steele worked quickly but methodically, to engineer a lingering, agonising death for one of his father's murderers. First he tied the groaning Binns to a doorpost of the stable. Then he rigged up a framework to the rear of the shack, fixing Binns' own rifle into it, carefully positioned so that it was aimed at the heart of the captive. A length of cord was tied to a thicker length of rope, the cord looped around the rifle trigger and it, and the rope, pulled taut and fixed to a nail.

After the knife wound had become numb, Binns began to plead for mercy, but Steele ignored his whining voice. His work almost finished, he went into the stable and back up to the hay-loft. He stretched out on the rotting straw and was able to drift into sleep, despite Binns' constant moaning.

He awoke at first light, and discovered that Binns had slipped into unconsciousness. The wound in the man's shoulder had festered. It looked ugly and it smelled of decay. There was water in a pool behind the stable and Steele scooped some up and saturated the rope.

Binns returned to awareness as the sun crested the horizon and struck him slantwise in the eyes. His shoulder seemed to be on fire. But he was able to forget his pain as he saw the first whisps of steam rising from the damp rope. He heard a sound at the side and snapped his head around, to see the impassive Steele leading the two horses from the stable. One was saddled. The other bolted when Steele slapped him hard on his flank.

'Why, mister?' Binns croaked.

'He was about run out,' Steele replied easily. 'This one's stronger.'

'You know I didn't mean that!' Binns screamed, on the verge of hysteria.

Steele ignored the question, as he lead the horse across the yard, checked the tension of the shrinking rope, then the aim of the rifle. He mounted.

'Why don't you just kill me?' Binns begged.

'Man ought to have time to make his peace with God,' Steele replied. 'My father was a religious man. He'd have wanted even his murderers to have that much.'

He clucked to the horse and walked the animal out of the yard. Behind him, Binns whimpered pathetically, then ceased abruptly as the rope creaked.

CHAPTER SEVENTEEN

FULLER'S Folly was constructed of roughcast stone and timber, designed in the shape of a European castle keep. It stood in the centre of a square area guarded by a twenty feet high wooden wall, thick enough for a sentry walkway to run along the top. There was a single gateway in the wall, wide enough to allow access to the largest wagon. Behind and to the sides of the fort, the terrain was a wasteland of jagged, sun-bleached rocks, scattered upon a vast area of unevenly convoluted ground – as if some gigantic explosion had ripped apart a mountain. At the front was a large, perfectly flat area, the furthest boundary marked by a flagpole from which flew the crossed and starred emblem of the Confederacy. Beyond this, the ground fell away sharply, the texture as harsh and grotesque as that of the terrain in every other direction.

The flag of the Confederate States was not the only banner waving limply in the slight morning breeze. For from a pole erected in front of the gates, the British Union Jack was wafted by the same breeze.

In the shadow of the pole stood a man of about sixty, tall, straight and with iron grey hair. He was still handsome, even though his face showed the many lines of his age. And his pale blue eyes were alert and bright, seeming strangely younger than his years. He was attired in the full uniform of a British army colonel, complete with ceremonial sword in a scabbard and a baton tucked under his arm.

Before him, on the drill square between the two flagpoles, six dark-skinned men dressed only in white loin-cloths and red scarves marched in two lines of three. Their movements were perfectly synchronised as they made turns, wheels and changes of pace in an excellent exhibition of precision marching. The officer remained silent throughout, a slight upturning of the corners of his mouth showing his enjoyment of the perfect display.

'Colonel! Colonel Fuller!'

The Indian natives continued to move across the drill square, like automatoms. The colonel's reaction to the interruption showed as a slight tic in his left cheek.

'Colonel!'

The tic became more rapid. Fuller continued to stand to rigid attention and his expression did not alter as he saw Carstairs come into view at the far side of the square. The younger Englishman was near exhaustion. He tried to break out into a run, but staggered and fell flat. He started to pick himself up.

'Detachment . . . halt!' Fuller roared.

The natives complied, standing stock still. Carstairs straightened, pulled back his shoulders and started off at a slow march. His steps faltered, but he struggled to retain some resemblance of military bearing.

'Detachment . . . left . . . turn!'

Again the natives moved as one, bare feet slapping against the rock like a single rifle shot. Carstairs reeled to a halt in front of Fuller and attempted to hold himself as rigid as the colonel. Fuller ignored him.

'Detachment . . . stand . . . at . . . ease!'

Bare feet cracked against rock once more. Fuller nodded his satisfaction, then swung his gaze towards the exhausted Carstairs. He swayed. The tic in the colonel's cheek twitched uncontrollably.

'Captain Carstairs reporting, sir,' Carstairs gasped, executing a salute, which threatened to topple him again. 'Washington mission accomplished. Enemy commander-in-chief mortally wounded. Union cavalry . . . cavalry troop . . . close at hand . . . sir.'

He turned and raised a hand to point to the far side of the drill square. But fatigue overcame him and he crumpled to the ground as the strength left his legs. The colonel stepped rapidly backwards, so that the unconscious man did not touch his highly-polished boots. Then he swung towards the natives and bellowed at them in rapid Urdu, his tic coming under control as the excitement at the prospect of action superceded his rage at the interruption of the drill routine.

Four of the natives did an about-face and ran to the far side of the square, disappearing over the rim. The remaining two loped forward and hoisted the limp form of Carstairs between them. They carried him in the wake of Fuller, who marched through the gateway and across the area within the stockade towards the main door of the fort. A further half dozen natives interrupted their fatigue duties and came to attention as Fuller marched into sight.

Inside, the Indians carried their burden up a broad stairway as Fuller turned into open double doors and closed them behind him. He took off his sword and set down his baton, then poured himself a whiskey from a decanter on a sideboard. He carried it to the side of a table which took up most of the floor-space in the room and sipped the liquor gratefully. His gleaming eyes roved over a contour map of the United States of America which had been built on the table. Countless small flags on pins were stuck into the map, a whole cluster of them on the spot marked WASHINGTON. Fuller removed four of these flags and set them down, then went to look out of a wide window. From it, he could see the Union Jack atop the flagpole beyond the stockade gates. As he watched, the breeze freshened and the flag began to fly with greater vigor. Fuller broadened his smile and raised his glass in a toast.

After he had finished his drink, he returned to the map table, picked up one of the discarded flags and pressed it into the point marked FORT FULLER. Then leaned his rump against the table and waited patiently for a full half hour before knuckles rapped on the door.

'Enter!' he called.

Carstairs came into the room, still weary, but looking better. He had bathed, shaved and donned the uniform of a British army captain. He stood to attention and saluted. 'I am now ready to make my report, sir.'

'At ease and easy, Captain,' Fuller instructed. 'What happened to your three men?'

'Killed by the enemy, sir,' Carstairs replied. 'They tracked us most of the way.' He shook his head, as if seeking to clear it of the after-effects of his arduous trek on foot. 'One of them – Logan – may have deserted under fire.'

Fuller waved his hand in a gesture of dismissal. 'Probably did, captain. Some of the riff-raff we've been forced to accept can't be trusted out of sight of an officer. But we'll simply post the man missing until we have confirmation. What is your estimation of the time it will take the enemy unit to reach our position?'

'Difficult to say, Colonel Fuller,' Carstairs replied. 'There's reason to believe they know of the existence of our position, but not the precise location.'

'Strength?'

'About a dozen.'

'Good. When they come, we'll be ready for them, eh? The more we can kill, the less there will be left to fight us in the big battle.'

'Yes, sir,' Carstairs acknowledged, able to conceal his relief. Although his mission had been successful, he had lost all his men and he had not been looking forward to seeing Fuller's reaction.

But there had been nothing to fear. Fuller was at a fever pitch of excitement as he turned to survey the map spread across the table. 'You did an excellent job, captain,' he congratulated, his back to Carstairs. 'With Lincoln dead and the country still reeling under the impact of this stupid civil war, the United States can be ours within a month. We'll show these people that they cannot stage mass revolution against the British Crown and live to enjoy what they term freedom. They may have stolen this land from George, but we will win it back for Victoria, eh what?'

Fuller whirled and stared at Carstairs, his eyes blazing with almost sexual enjoyment. Carstairs came smartly to attention and saluted. 'God bless her!' he snapped.

'Amen to that,' Fuller agreed. 'Now go and rest, captain. You will be roused when the enemy are sighted. It will be good to fight in a skirmish again, eh?'

'Even better then the counter-revolution begins, sir.'

Fuller nodded gleefully. 'Quite right, captain. We'll show the old country how wrong it was about us.'

When Carstairs had about-faced and marched from the room, Fuller poured himself another whiskey and returned to the vantage point of the window. Because of the sudden falling away of the ground beyond the drill square, he was unable to see anything but blue sky on the other side of the pole flying the flag of the Confederacy.

And, in his turn, Adam Steele could see only the pole and pennant at the top of the rugged slope he was climbing. His progress was slow, because his horse was almost spent and he proceeded on foot, leading the lathered animal by the bridle. There was no marked trail and he followed the easiest route, around monolithic rock formations and skirting treacherous, deep slashes in the ground.

It was as he rounded a massive boulder that one of the natives leapt into his path, drawing a knife from his loincloth. Steele froze for a second, ready to fling himself to the side if the Indian hurled the knife. The man merely brandished the weapon, a sly grin decorating his dark-skinned features.

Steele swept the presentation rifle from the saddle boot and levelled it. 'Drop it, feller,' he said softly.

A swishing sound distracted him and his eyes swivelled. In the next instant, a silk scarf, weighted at the ends, looped around his throat and was pulled tight. He felt hot breath against his ear.

'You drop gun,' a voice whispered, speaking English with a strange accent. 'You struggle, me pull tighter. You understand, damn Yankee?'

Two more Indians moved out into the open, flanking the one with the knife. They wore the same kind of grins. One of them beckoned. The scarf around Steele's neck was threatening to choke him. He contemplated swinging around, placing the man at his back between himself and the three black men. But he decided the one with the knife would be too fast for him. He held the rifle across his chest, then tossed it to the man who had beckoned. It was caught, expertly checked, then aimed at him. The scarf was pulled clear of Steele's neck and he rubbed the red mark it had left on his skin. He glanced over his shoulder and saw a fourth Indian grinning at him.

'Where's the cooking pot?' he asked wryly.

The man in back of him was replacing the scarf around his own neck, crossing the weighted ends to keep it in place. He looked up at Steele with shocked eyes. 'Goodness gracious, we no eat white man,' he exclaimed. 'We Christian British subjects. You come with us – not escape?'

'What if I try?' Steele suggested, fingering the ornate head of the tiepin in his neckerchief and making an effort to keep his legs straight so that the slit in the seam would not show.

'Then you die,' the spokesman for the natives replied simply.

'There's a lot of that about,' Steele commented sardonically, and started to walk in the direction indicated by the man with his rifle.

The gates in the stockade wall had been closed by the time the prisoner and escort had reached the top of the slope. But they were swung wide as the group crossed the drill square.

Steele's features were as impassive as usual as he surveyed the scene in front of the incongruous castle keep. A table had been set up a few yards in front of the main doorway and Colonel Fuller sat on a chair to one side, drinking tea from a bone china cup. Cool shadow was provided by a multi-coloured sunshade held over him by an Indian. A second Indian was unloading a plate of daintily cut sandwiches from a silver salver on to the table.

The British officer's reaction was as low-keyed as that of Steele as he watched the prisoner and escort approach, then halt before him.

'Beg the colonel's pardon. No soldiers come. But this one civilian. He act like he up to no good, sir.'

Fuller finished drinking his tea, placed the cup down carefully in its matching saucer, then regarded Steele with a steady gaze. 'Name, rank and serial number?' he demanded.

The natives were standing to rigid attention. Steele's slouching stance was in keeping with his disheveled appearance. 'Name's Steele,' he answered easily. 'Used to be a lieutenant.'

The tic became a twitch in the colonel's cheek. 'You're with Union intelligence!' he accused.

Steele shook his head. 'I'm with me.'

'And he's come to see me, sir.'

The natives continued to stare directly ahead. Fuller and Steele both looked towards the deep shadows within the doorway. The American's mouthline tightened almost imperceptibly as he recognised the uniformed figure who stepped through into the sunlight.

'You know this man, Captain Carstairs?' Fuller snapped.

'I think I may have met somebody related to him, sir,' Carstairs replied, fixing Steele with a triumphant stare.

'I'd be obliged if you would stop talking in riddles, captain!'

Steele saw the muscular spasms in the older man's face begin to get agitated and recognised it as a sign of rising temper. 'Don't burst your breeches, colonel,' he said coolly. 'The captain and three of his buddies lynched my father for the sheer hell of it. The others have already paid. I don't figure to let this guy get away with it.'

Fuller continued to stare angrily at Carstairs for several moments, then turned his fury towards Steele. 'The three men under Captain Carstairs' command were killed in action with Union cavalry,' he rasped.

Steele shrugged. 'I'm not calling him a liar if he told you that, colonel. But maybe the captain was running so hard he didn't have the time to look back and see what was really happening.'

'Sir, I – '

Fuller whirled towards Carstairs so fast he almost toppled his chair. 'Silence!' he roared. He struggled to calm himself. 'Tiffin is no time for arguments.' He nodded to the native holding the tray and the man stepped forward and poured fresh tea from a silver pot. Fuller picked up a quarter sandwich and nibbled at it. His voice became calm. 'Captain Carstairs and the three brave men who died serving the cause carried out a faultless operation. They are to be congratulated on the manner in which they stirred up an element anxious to overthrow the Washington administration but lacking that final spur of action.

'But now we can disassociate ourselves from such people. They were merely undisciplined civilians who saw no further than the single act which satisfied their spiteful intent.'

He sipped his tea and seemed to expect a comment from Steele. When the American failed to break his silence, Fuller continued.

'In a war, it is inevitable that some innocent people will suffer, others will die. But, in the end, all sacrifices will be justified.' He raised his teacup, as if it were a wine glass, in an informal toast. 'I drink to Captain Carstairs; to the Confederacy for their great struggle over five long years to weaken and demoralise those who held power in Washington; and to the many thousands of men throughout the country who answered my call to partake in a victory that was denied them in the secessionist cause – but which will undoubtedly be fulfilled as part of the British Army of Liberation.'

Under normal circumstances, Steele might have given consideration to the sanity of the colonel, with his bellowing voice and the blazing eyes. He might have wondered if the man's words were the ravings of a megalomaniac or a declaration of intent with valid support. But everything Fuller said washed over and around Steele as the American fixed Carstairs with a level stare, heavily menacing in its complete lack of emotion.

Fuller seemed about to launch into a further discourse on his plans to win back the United States for the British crown. But a shout from the walkway above the gate halted him. Fuller looked through, and across the drill square, his excitement dying; to be replaced by a gentle smile of quiet pleasure.

'Ah, visitors,' he said, then used his rapid Urdu to give orders to the natives, who all broke away and ran, some into the castle, others across the compound to climb the stockade walls.

Steele glanced over his shoulder and saw the much depleted cavalry troop crossing the drill square. Only the lieutenant, sergeant, and three superficially wounded troopers were mounted. The rest – numbering six – marched in a column.

'Take the prisoner downstairs, Captain,' Fuller instructed. 'We have more pressing business to attend to at the moment.'

When Steele turned around, he found himself looking down the barrel of a Colt revolver clutched in Carstairs' well-manicured right hand. The young Englishman was smiling in triumph.

'But don't harm him,' Fuller instructed. Carstairs' expression darkened, but then showed approval at the colonel's next comment. 'The thuggees need some strenuous exercise, and we have not had a hunt for such a long time.'

Carstairs gestured with the revolver and Steele stepped forward, crossing the threshold into the dark coolness of the castle keep.

As Steele went from sight, Carey led his unit in through the open gateway and halted his horse, his tired eyes growing wide with amazement as he saw the British officer calmly sipping tea and eating sandwiches at the now unshaded table.

'What the hell . . . '. the sergeant exclaimed softly.

'Welcome, lieutenant!' Fuller called warmly. 'Please bring your men inside and join me for tiffin.'

Carey struggled to overcome his surprise. He cleared his throat and tried to inject a note of authority into his voice. 'I must ask you to strike the Confederate colours, sir,' he called.

'At sunset,' Fuller acknowledged, then raised his voice and emitted a gutteral sound.

This was, in fact, an order for the thuggees. There was a strange rumbling sound which seemed to come from the sky. Several of the troopers glanced curiously up at the blue void, expecting to see suddenly formed thunder clouds.

'Christ!' the sergeant gasped, reaching for his rifle.

He did not get it clear of the boot. A ball from one of the four 12-pounders which had been rolled to the edge of the castle keep roof decapitated him and became buried in the chest of the trooper standing behind him.

Every other man in the troop fixed the roof with a terrified stare, frozen into an instant of immobility as they saw the black smoke whirling from the muzzle. Then the three other artillery pieces roared. One man's leg was shot off at the knee. Another was flung violently from his saddle, a gaping hole in his stomach where a ball had passed clean through him. A third stared down in disbelief at his dismembered arm as it fell to the ground. A fourth toppled sideways, then crawled around with tears streaming down his young face. He peered over the edge of a hole in the ground and reached inside it.

Colonel Fuller watched the carnage over the rim of his teacup and made no move to rise from the table as the survivors of the barrage shook free of their immobilising horror and drew their guns.

The young trooper who had fallen succeeded in freeing something from beneath the ballshot at the bottom of the hole. It was the front half of his right boot. The crushed bones and pulped flesh of half his right foot was inside it. He smelled the blood and fainted.

Before the troopers could squeeze off a single shot, they were attacked for a second time; and again, death rained on them from above. This time it took the form of eight thuggees, dropping down from the walkway above the gate. Some landed lightly on their feet and lunged into the attack with flashing knives and whirling scarves. Others smashed down on to terrified troopers, plunging knives into their chests or slinging scarves around pulsing throats and jerking hard at the weighted ends.

They killed in complete silence, grinning broadly at each spurt of blood or sigh of stale air forced from dead lungs. Only three shots were fired by the troopers, all wild, the triggers of pistols and rifles squeezed by dying fingers. Those soldiers wounded by the artillery fire were shown no more mercy than the uninjured. So that, within thirty seconds, silence returned to the compound. The thuggees padded away on their bare feet, leaving behind them a ghastly pile of sprawled bodies; some with only a red weal on their throats; others dripping blood from terrible mutilations.

'Well done, men!' Fuller bellowed as the thuggees formed into ranks before the tea table and came to attention. 'That is only a foretaste of what is required of you. I have no doubt that we will succeed in our purpose.'

At the foot of a dank staircase beneath the castle keep, Steele and Carstairs heard the colonel's excited voice end the silence which had succeeded the screams of the dying troopers. Carstairs waved the revolver towards an open doorway and Steele went through, into a rank smelling room with walls, floor and ceiling of solid rock. A thick wooden door with a small barred aperture in it, was slammed closed. Two bolts were shot.

The Englishman had allowed him not the slightest opportunity to escape. In the near pitch blackness of the underground cell, he neither felt nor showed any despondency over this.

'Didn't take long, did it?' Carstairs said gleefully. 'Those thuggees are quite something, aren't they?'

Steele fingered his throat, still showing the mark of the scarf which had threatened to throttle him. 'They're just a pain in the neck,' he replied wryly.

CHAPTER EIGHTEEN

IT was eight o'clock the next morning when the stout door was flung open and three thuggees confronted Steele. One held a Henry rifle and the others balanced knives in their brown skinned hands, making it evident that they were prepared to hurl the blades at the slightest provocation.

'You come with us,' the man with the rifle ordered.

Steele had slept the entire night and felt mentally rested. But the rock floor had been singularly lacking in comfort and his muscles were stiff. The walk up the stairway and across the compound loosened them a little. And the warm sunlight of morning extracted the chillness from his flesh.

The castle keep and area inside the stockade was in the grip of a strong silence. The bodies of the troopers had been removed from the gateway and there was only a scattering of dark stains as evidence of the massacre that had taken place there.

Steele ambled along in front of his escorts: and yet again, his strength of purpose and determination to take his revenge on the last of his father's murderers, negated any surprise he might have felt at the scene on the drill square.

Carstairs and Fuller were sitting astride handsome chestnut horses. Both men were attired in hunting pink, complete with hard black hats. The colonel held a brass hunting horn. Carstairs caught the rifle thrown to him by the thuggee and pointed it at Steele. The thuggees who had brought the prisoner up from the dungeon cell scuttled over to join their fellow countrymen standing at ease behind the mounted officers.

'Pink's definitely your colour, Carstairs,' Steele said sardonically.

'It tones well with the yellow streak down your back.'

Carstairs scowled and changed the aim of the rifle, drawing a bead on Steele's head.

'Now now, captain!' Fuller chided. 'Shooting the quarry in cold blood is no sport for officers and gentlemen.'

'I'm the prey, uh?' Steele asked.

'You should spell it with an *a* and do it,' Carstairs put in sourly.

Fuller's expression and tone became stern. 'Captain Carstairs gave me a full report of the events in Washington, Steele. He killed your father in the execution of his duty to our cause. It was necessary in order to confuse the enemy. However, you have my admiration for the manner in which you have sought to avenge his death.' He nodded, agreeing with himself. Then he cleared his throat. 'Whether the captain failed to realise you killed the men – rather than the army – because of cowardice or erroneous judgement is a matter of opinion. I choose to believe the latter.'

'For me, it makes no difference, I guess,' Steele replied.

'That is correct. You did what you considered to be your duty. And, as such, you cannot be faulted. But neither can you be allowed to go unpunished for your interference with our cause.' He beamed suddenly. 'I am a man who believes in making the punishment fit the crime.' There was another abrupt switch in his mood, and he became sullen. 'Unfortunately, the army authorities in India saw fit to take me to task for such a belief. But I intend to show you. You hunted down my men and killed them. Now you will be hunted down and killed.'

'Sounds like fun,' Steele muttered.

Fuller beamed again. 'You will be given a reasonable head start. Most of the enjoyment is in the chase, eh what? The kill is merely the climax of all else. Now run, Steele – for your very life.'

Steele touched the brim of his hat. 'I'm grateful to you, colonel,' he said, then turned and broke into a loping run, heading for one corner of the stockade wall.

'Excellent day for a hunt, captain,' Fuller commented, standing in the stirrups and glancing around at the barren terrain bathed in the gentle warmth of morning sunshine.

'Topping, sir,' Carstairs agreed, concentrating his attention upon the high ground above the rear of the fort.

He saw Steele once, fleetingly, darting out from behind a boulder and then going from sight beyond the tesselated roof of the castle keep with the cannons still in position.

Steele did not concern himself with backward glances. The rising ground was steeper than it looked – and more rugged. The single night of long, undisturbed sleep in the discomfort of the cell had achieved a little in restoring the energy which had drained from him throughout the chase. But the effort necessary to put space between himself and the men on the drill square soon negated its effect.

Not until he had crested the first major rise did he sink down and roll over to peer back the way he had come. The incongruous castle with its waving flags and the men ranged up in front of it looked like toys from such a height. But they were deadly playthings, and this was no game. Sunlight flashed on metal, and the shrill blast of the hunting horn drifted through the heat haze hanging over the barren terrain.

The brown skinned men in loincloths and scarves streamed off the drill square in an orderly run, then scattered as they advanced up the incline.

'*Tally-ho!*

Fuller's voice, travelling over such a distance, had a childlike quality about it. But he urged his horse forward into a canter with the skill of an expert. Carstairs was only yards behind him.

Steele checked the weapons the thuggees and British officers had not thought to look for. The knife rested snugly in the boot sheath; the derringer, with a single shot left, nestled in the pocket of his sheepskin coat. He fingered the ornate head of the tiepin. Then he rose into a crouch and raked the scattering of rocks on a level area before the ground took an upward incline again.

He settled on a cluster of boulders at the foot of the new slope and raced towards them, knowing he could not be seen by the men clambering up from below. He sank into the the snug pocket of cover provided by the rocks and squatted down to wait.

Two thuggees crested the rise together, and split up, going to left and right. The hunting horn blasted, much closer than before. Three more thuggees leapt into view. Two went to the left. The other loped in the direction of Steele's hiding place. He slowed as he drew nearer, recognising it's possibility for cover. Then, abruptly, he made a running jump into the rocks, his knife ready for a lethal slash.

He was in mid-air when he saw Steele. He struggled to turn his body, to be in a position to attack when he landed. But Steele moved further to the side, his fingers snatching the tiepin free of the neckerchief. Six inches of pointed metal glinted, then streaked forward. The thuggee hit the ground and gave a gasp of horror. The pin pierced the side of his neck and penetrated to its full length. Blood from the punctured jugular vein gushed from his mouth as he fell.

'Bad way to go, but I guess you're stuck with it,' Steele muttered as he withdrew the pin.

The two mounted officers crested the rise only feet behind a group of panting thuggees. Fuller, his eyes blazing, gave another blast on the horn. Carstairs changed his grip on the Henry repeater, holding it by the barrel. He crashed the stock across the back of one of the stragglers.

'Find him, you lazy buggers!' he shrieked.

The thuggees raced across the flat ground and up the new slope. The Englishmen galloped their horses on ahead. Three thuggees approached the rocks in which Steele was crouched. One went either side as the third clambered up and over.

The hunting horn wailed. Steele jerked out the derringer and sent a shot smashing into the heart of the man on the rocks. Only the men close to him heard the shot against the cry of the horn. Both turned towards Steele, one with a knife, the second whirling his scarf.

Steele's hand streaked to his boot. His own knife came free. He hurled it, underhand, and the thuggee's weapon spun away as he grasped at the handle of Steele's knife, which seemed to be growing from his belly. Steele leapt clear of the man's falling body, pivoting as he did so and swinging a clenched fist.

The third thuggee was lunging at him, whirling the weighted scarf above his head. He saw the fist rocketing towards him and tried to parry the blow. But Steele pulled the punch, and raked his arm to right and left. The world went black for the thuggee as the point of the tiepin, protruding between Steele's clenched fingers, slashed across both eyes, blinding him. He fell to his knees and wailed, his hands becoming covered with blood as he rubbed at his sliced eyes.

There was no blast of the hunting horn to conceal this sound. Steele heard a shout and whirled to look up the slope. He saw Carstairs in the process of wheeling his mount and knew the Englishman had seen him.

He leapt clear of the rocks and raced across the flat area towards the top of the lower slope. He slid over the edge and pressed himself flat, cursing. His knife was still buried in the stomach of one of the thuggees. He had dropped the tiepin on the run and the derringer was empty.

He heard the thunder of galloping hooves and rolled over on to his back under the lip of the hill top. His eyes swivelled upwards to their fullest extent. He saw the head of the horse, then the fore-legs. Carstairs boots in the stirrups came into view. Steele launched himself upright, arms reaching, hands clawed. In that split second, Carstairs saw him: excitement of anticipation becoming pleasure of the act. He aimed the rifle to fire.

Steele caught the barrel in a two handed grip and jerked. The horse was committed to its leap over the edge of the rise. Neither man was prepared to release his grip on the rifle: until Carstairs was snatched bodily from the saddle. The Englishman screamed and flailed his arms and legs, seeking a way to break his fall.

His hands hit the rocky ground first. The impact snapped his arms at the wrists and elbows and gleaming white bone burst through flesh in great spurts of scarlet blood. His body smashed down. The scream became a groan and he rolled his head over to stare in horror at Steele.

'All the way, you've been riding for a fall,' Steele said, turning the rifle.

He shot Carstairs in the side of the head from a range of only inches. The Englishman's brains sizzled in a dozen steaming blobs on the hot rocks.

'Did you get him, captain?'

Fuller's voice held a note of disappointment. It warned Steele not to waste time in regret that Carstairs had died so quickly. He turned and flung himself to the ground, then bellied up the slope until he could see across the flat area. Fuller was walking his horse across the small plain, accompanied by eight thuggees, flanking him, four on each side.

Steele waited until they were in the centre of the open ground, then went up on to one knee. Fuller halted his horse, and the entire side of his face twitched in hot fury. The thuggees looked at their commander for orders. Steele squeezed the trigger and pumped the action, squeezed the trigger and pumped the action. Eight times. Each shot was carefully placed, into the heart of an unmoving thuggee.

When the last man pitched to the ground, Fuller allowed the hunting horn to fall and raised his hands.

'It is not in my nature to order a retreat,' he said. 'And they would not like to have died whilst running away.'

Steele pumped the repeater, slotting a bullet into the breech. 'One man who lived by the sword is going to perish by something else,' he said softly.

Fuller brought his tic under control. 'I should like it to be with dignity,' he replied.

CHAPTER NINETEEN

ADAM Steele stood in the gateway of the stockade wall, the walkway casting a deep shadow across him. The tiepin was back in his neckerchief, but was hidden by the weighted scarf he had taken from one of the dead thuggees. The knife had been replaced in the boot sheath, the empty derringer was in his coat pocket and the presentation rifle was in his hands, levelled towards the base of the flagpole on the fort side of the drill square.

Colonel Fuller, in full dress uniform complete with sword, stood at the side of the pole, slowly hauling down the Union Jack. When the flag had settled into the dust, he came to attention, did an about-face, drew his sword and marched towards Steele. The American kept the Colt Hartford aimed steadily at the Englishman. Both men's faces were blank.

Fuller halted, raised a knee and snapped the sword cleanly in half. He dropped both sections to the ground and came to attention again.

'Thank you for that,' he said calmly. 'Now you may shoot. The plan will die with me.'

Steele nodded and adjusted the angle of the rifle, to send a bullet into the man's heart. But before he could squeeze the trigger, another gun exploded. Fuller's eyes closed and he pitched forward, legs still together, arms stiff at his sides. As he measured his length of the ground, Steele saw the blood-pumping hole in the back of his head.

Steele looked up, and across the drill square. Bishop and Lovell sat astride their horses on the far side. There was a smoking rifle in the hands of the frock-coated Washington detective. The deputy's hand still rested on the barrel from where he had spoiled Lovell's shot. Three men on foot stood beside the mounted law officers.

'Looks like I've got to start believing in ghosts,' Steele called as the group moved slowly towards him.

The men on foot were Logan, Monahan and Binns. Monahan hobbled painfully on his injured leg. Binns' arm was in a sling.

'They're alive, Adam,' Bishop said. 'I told you I'd be behind you the whole way.'

Steele nodded. 'I should have believed you, Bish,' he acknowledged. 'You always were a man of your word.'

He had no way of knowing who Lovell was. But he recognised the detective's expression – naked hatred.

'Me, too, Steele,' Lovell snarled. 'I promised I'd kill you when I found out you burned my brother.'

Bishop snapped his head around to stare at Lovell. 'So that's why you were so damn set on – '

'There's three more of us got reason to want you dead, Steele,' Monahan spat.

'My father . . . Binns' brother . . . this guy's brother. Lot of relative killing.'

The group halted, about twenty feet in front of the shadowed gateway where Steele stood.

'You ready to come back, Adam?' Bishop asked.

'You'll never get him there, deputy,' Lovell snapped. 'I aim to teach this bastard a lesson.'

'I've already learned one,' Steele said easily, recalling the way Carstairs had died.

'How's that?' Lovell asked suspiciously.

'If you intend to kill a man, do it quick,' Steele rapped out.

As he finished speaking, he went into a crouch, bringing up the rifle. The first shot burrowed into Lovell's heart, lifting him from the saddle. The rifle cracked three more times. Monahan, Logan and Binns staggered back and toppled, blood fountaining from ghastly head wounds.

Bishop had to calm his frightened horse before he could draw a bead on Steele, but by then the Colt Hartford was aimed straight at him. The young deputy was certain he was about to die and there was deep regret in his eyes as he matched the steady stare of his childhood friend. Then, abruptly, Steele smiled and pointed his rifle towards the sky. He squeezed the trigger and the hammer struck an expended cartridge.

EDGE: THE LONER

by George G. Gilman

First in a new Western series whose hero is the lone and sinister Edge – a new kind of Western hero, a man alone.

The idealised Westerner lives clean, is respectful to ladies, courteous to his social inferiors and gives his enemies a sporting chance.

Edge is not an idealised Westerner – not in any way at all.

Look out for Edge.

NEW ENGLISH LIBRARY

EDGE:
TEN THOUSAND DOLLARS, AMERICAN

by George G. Gilman

Second in a new Western series, this story is set South of the Border where men live miserably and die violently.

Ten American dollars can keep a family for months. For ten thousand dollars a man would slit the throat of his own grandmother.

Edge knows where such a sum is hidden and the bandits know that he knows. The shadow of death hangs over them all.

NEW ENGLISH LIBRARY

26A EDGE TEN THOUSAND

T011 682	ESCAPE ON VENUS	*Edgar Rice Burroughs*	40p
T013 537	WIZARD OF VENUS	*Edgar Rice Burroughs*	30p
T009 696	GLORY ROAD	*Robert Heinlein*	40p
T010 856	THE DAY AFTER TOMORROW	*Robert Heinlein*	30p
T016 900	STRANGER IN A STRANGE LAND	*Robert Heinlein*	75p
T011 844	DUNE	*Frank Herbert*	75p
T012 298	DUNE MESSIAH	*Frank Herbert*	40p
T015 211	THE GREEN BRAIN	*Frank Herbert*	30p

War

T013 367	DEVIL'S GUARD	*Robert Elford*	50p
T013 324	THE GOOD SHEPHERD	*C. S. Forester*	35p
T011 755	TRAWLERS GO TO WAR	*Lund & Ludlam*	40p
T015 505	THE LAST VOYAGE OF GRAF SPEE	*Michael Powell*	30p
T015 661	JACKALS OF THE REICH	*Ronald Seth*	30p
T012 263	FLEET WITHOUT A FRIEND	*John Vader*	30p

Western

T016 994	No. 1 EDGE – THE LONER	*George G. Gilman*	30p
T016 986	No. 2 EDGE – TEN THOUSAND DOLLARS AMERICAN	*George G. Gilman*	30p
T017 613	No. 3 EDGE – APACHE DEATH	*George G. Gilman*	30p
T017 001	No. 4 EDGE – KILLER'S BREED	*George G. Gilman*	30p
T016 536	No. 5 EDGE – BLOOD ON SILVER	*George G. Gilman*	30p
T017 621	No. 6 EDGE – THE BLUE, THE GREY AND THE RED	*George G. Gilman*	30p
T014 479	No. 7 EDGE – CALIFORNIA KILLING	*George G. Gilman*	30p
T015 254	No. 8 EDGE – SEVEN OUT OF HELL	*George G. Gilman*	30p
T015 475	No. 9 EDGE – BLOODY SUMMER	*George G. Gilman*	30p
T015 769	No. 10 EDGE – VENGEANCE IS BLACK	*George G. Gilman*	30p

General

T011 763	SEX MANNERS FOR MEN	*Robert Chartham*	30p
W002 531	SEX MANNERS FOR ADVANCED LOVERS	*Robert Chartham*	25p
W002 835	SEX AND THE OVER FORTIES	*Robert Chartham*	30p
T010 732	THE SENSUOUS COUPLE	*Dr. 'C'*	25p

Mad

S004 708	VIVA MAD!	30p
S004 676	MAD'S DON MARTIN COMES ON STRONG	30p
S004 816	MAD'S DAVE BERG LOOKS AT SICK WORLD	30p
S005 078	MADVERTISING	30p
S004 987	MAD SNAPPY ANSWERS TO STUPID QUESTIONS	30p

NEL P.O. BOX 11, FALMOUTH, TR10 9EN, CORNWALL

Please send cheque or postal order. Allow 10p to cover postage and packing on one book plus 4p for each additional book.

Name ....

Address...

....

Title ....

(SEPTEMBER)